W9-CTH-318

INTENT TO KILL

Mrs. Beck felt suddenly fierce and righteous. She firmed her hand on the doorknob. "If the madman is in our cellar," she said, "he has *no business* there." She yanked open the door. The only thing in her mind was I'll have to see. I'll have to see.

Then she felt the force on her back, the flat hand pushing, violently. She tried, too late, to catch her footing, but the cellar steps were steep and went almost directly down. She felt the first shock, as her shoulder hit the stone of a step, and the second, as her arm bent wrong. And then, in pain, she tumbled on. She felt no shock at all, from the hard stone floor . . .

MASTERWORKS OF MYSTERY
BY MARY ROBERTS RINEHART!

THE YELLOW ROOM (2262, $3.50)

The somewhat charred corpse unceremoniously stored in the linen closet of Carol Spencer's Maine summer home set the plucky amateur sleuth on the trail of a killer. But each step closer to a solution led Carol closer to her own imminent demise!

THE CASE OF JENNIE BRICE (2193, $2.95)

The bloodstained rope, the broken knife—plus the disappearance of lovely Jennie Brice—were enough to convince Mrs. Pittman that murder had been committed in her boarding house. And if the police couldn't see what was in front of their noses, then the inquisitive landlady would just have to take matters into her own hands!

THE GREAT MISTAKE (2122, $3.50)

Patricia Abbott never planned to fall in love with wealthy Tony Wainwright, especially after she found out about the wife he'd never bothered to mention. But suddenly she was trapped in an extra-marital affair that was shadowed by unspoken fear and shrouded in cold, calculating murder!

THE RED LAMP (2017, $3.50)

The ghost of Uncle Horace was getting frisky—turning on lamps, putting in shadowy appearances in photographs. But the mysterious nightly slaughter of local sheep seemed to indicate that either Uncle Horace had developed a bizarre taste for lamb chops . . . or someone was manipulating appearances with a deadly sinister purpose!

A LIGHT IN THE WINDOW (1952, $3.50)

Ricky Wayne felt uncomfortable about moving in with her new husband's well-heeled family while he was overseas fighting the Germans. But she never imagined the depths of her in-laws' hatred—or the murderous lengths to which they would go to break up her marriage!

Available wherever paperbacks are sold, or order direct from the Publisher. Send cover price plus 50¢ per copy for mailing and handling to Zebra Books, Dept. 3346, 475 Park Avenue South, New York, N.Y. 10016. Residents of New York, New Jersey and Pennsylvania must include sales tax. DO NOT SEND CASH.

CHARLOTTE ARMSTRONG

THE TURRET ROOM

ZEBRA BOOKS
KENSINGTON PUBLISHING CORP.

ZEBRA BOOKS

are published by

Kensington Publishing Corp.
475 Park Avenue South
New York, NY 10016

Copyright © 1965 by Charlotte Armstrong. Published by arrangement with the Jack and Charlotte Lewi Family Trust.

All rights reserved. No part of this book may be reproduced in any form or by any means without the prior written consent of the Publisher, excepting brief quotes used in reviews.

First Zebra Books printing: March, 1991

Printed in the United States of America

Chapter One

His feet were lumps of pain. The foot he had once broken ached a little deeper than the other, which put an accent on the rhythm, LEFT right LEFT right, but there was not enough difference to make him limp. In fact, he was striding along pretty good, pretty good, but he knew that he had better not break his stride or he might not get going again. His head was light. He fancied that he was riding on a wheel. Well, it had been too much, it had been too far, it had been a stupid thing to do, to walk all the way, but he could not stop, now.

The last time he had stopped, when was that, about four miles ago, the other edge of town, to put on his clean white orderly's coat in the gas station, to shave, to wash his face and hands, to comb his hair, he had been tempted to take a bus, but he had known, even then, that he could get himself going about once more, and that would be all. And no bus came nearer than half a mile to the big house on the knoll.

He guessed it was afternoon, the third day he had been walking. The first day had been so fine. On the morning of the second day, he had been pretty

5

stiff, pretty sore, but he'd walked that off and been pleased with himself. *This* day had been bad, all the way. Psyche and soma, he thought. I'm trying to fool myself into aches and pains, because some of me wants to give up. I'm getting there. And I'm getting scared.

It was a nice street he was on. He had always thought so. It was the older part of the little town. There were big trees. All the houses were big houses. Nobody walked. There were no children playing in the yards. There must be children, he thought, but each child has his own little paradise around at the back. If there are any children . . .

He was getting there, but his heart was too tired to beat any faster when he turned in at the drive where the old iron gates stood open, as they always had, as he remembered. He dared not stop, but just as he made the turn he lifted his right arm and sent the little canvas carrying-bag sailing into the juniper bushes.

He had his pride. He had walked some seventy-odd miles in two days and a little more than half a day, LEFT right LEFT right, all the way, and he was going to make it, but he would not even seem to suggest that he stay. He was hot and he was very tired, but he had washed, and put on the only clean garment that he had. He would do now what he had to do, partly because he was afraid to do it, and then he would take the bus back up North, and begin the new life.

There it was, the house with the tower. It wasn't much of a tower. It was too low, nothing but a rounded turret, half embedded, half protruding, but it had the little slitty windows that you see in pictures of castles. The tower was stone, and the house was stucco, gray, the color of stone. But the roof was red tile and the ground floor went slopping over the ground horizontally, with shutters on the windows. The main part had been built (he seemed to know) by Wendy's great-grandfather and the wing at the right added on by her grandfather. One of them, probably the first one, had planted the tree.

It was a rubber tree, or some such thing, and it had sure grown, he thought. Sure grown. It stood smack in the middle of the big arched window at the front of the house, and it spread, it snubbed against the tower, it spread its upper limbs over the tower, it had shed huge leathery leaves on the tiles, on the ground, all around. So it stood, like a huge plume, an outburst of natural laughter, ignoring the facade of the house.

Harold Page put his leaden feet down, one after the other, until he came up to the big wooden door with its ornate iron hinges. He lifted his leaden arm and his wooden finger found the bell.

Before he had to ring again, the big door was opened by a girl and she wasn't Wendy. She wasn't anyone he had ever seen before. She didn't look as if she belonged here. She was a pretty girl, about twenty-four or twenty-five, he thought, and she was wearing black capris, neat and tight but not too tight, and a pale pink tailored blouse. Her hair was a pale yellow, smooth, and drawn back, held by a

7

pale pink band, and her gray eyes immediately winced with alarm.

"You're . . . not from the hospital!" she said to him.

He could hardly lift his tongue. He could hardly think. He was feeling a bitter disappointment. He was thinking, They don't live here anymore. His voice came out in tired gasps. "That's right. The Whitmans? They . . . live here?"

The girl said, "Well, *of course. Yes.* What *is* it?" Her neat flat black slippers took a step backward upon the dark brown tile, and Harold stumbled forward. The cool and faintly stale air of the house hit him; he almost fell.

"Walked . . . all the way," he mumbled. "So hot . . . Excuse me."

The girl said, "You'd better come in. It's always cool in here."

I know, he thought. I know. She seemed to shepherd him across the narrow foyer to the arch and the two steps down into the big room that was just exactly as he had remembered it. He slid his feet cautiously on the slippery tile steps, until they hit the carpet, and there he stood. The ceiling was still very high, the walls still looked like yellow stone, the velvets on the big chairs were the same, some gold, some a faded rose. And the turret wall still invaded the room's huge rectangle, with the stairs still winding up around its gentle curve. The floor of this room was below the level of the ground outside the huge window, and there was the tree, seen from within, overpowering, its great bare trunk rising from a knot of gnarled roots, its leaves pushing

8

at the upper window within the peak of the Spanish arch of the glass, shutting the house away from the sky and turning its ancient, expensive austerity in upon itself.

It was very cool in here.

But now this modern-looking girl said urgently, "Did anything happen?" Just as he had brought himself to ask, "Is Mr. Whitman here?"

He couldn't talk over her, he hadn't the energy. In fact, he wasn't sure how much longer he could even stand. But she let him speak.

"Or Mrs. Whitman? Or old Mrs. Whitman?" Any of them, he was thinking, but I had better not ask for Wendy.

"Well, none of them are here just now," she said, in a different voice, a careful voice. "I'm Edith Thompson. I'm a kind of poor relation. Hey, you'd better sit down."

He guessed he had better, before he fell down, so he staggered as far as the first big chair and fell into it. Now his back was to the window and the tree. The girl came, treading lightly and softly, moving with easy grace, around him and the chair, to face him.

"Excuse me," he apologized. "My legs just don't . . . want to hold me up." The light was falling coolly and steadily upon her and he thought he could guess something. "You must be related to Mrs. Whitman. Myra, I mean." His voice sounded draggy and dreary. He was glad of this respite, though. She would let him wait, and by the time anybody came, he would be feeling much better.

But the girl said, crinkling up her eyes so that her

small straight nose seemed to sharpen with suspicion, "Why do you say that?"

"You have the same color hair. I thought . . . maybe . . . You look a little bit like her . . ." He was rambling.

The girl took her breath in, and smiled. "Do I?" she said in a friendly fashion. "No, I'm related to old Mrs. Whitman." She sat down on the ottoman.

"Granny?" he muttered. He couldn't pay attention. He was beginning to drift. The deadness of the air, the softness of the chair, this hiatus between the end of the journey and its objective. . . . He had better pull himself together. So he said, as briskly as he could, "Excuse me. It's not very polite to fall apart like this. But it sure was a long long walk and today was the worst. Turned so hot. Will they be back soon? Please?"

The girl just looked at him. He seemed to be able to see her mind turning around to remember the first words she had said to him. "From the *hospital!*" she exclaimed. "You don't mean you've walked all the way from *that* hospital? You *are* Harold Page, aren't you?"

"Didn't I say? I'm sorry." (Surely, he had said.) "I don't know what's the matter with me," he continued truthfully.

"Would you like a glass of water?" She was half up; her whole impulse was to be kind.

"Oh, I sure would," he sighed, "if it's not . . . too much . . . trouble . . ." His lips were feeling thick, now, and his mouth very dry. He heard her say something about Mrs. Beck lying down, she would get it, he must rest a minute, and he mumbled

10

something. Then she was gone and he was all alone, and he shivered.

Almost two years since he had been here. Very bad years. Or very good, who could say? He had learned a lot. He was twenty-one years old, now — not such a boy, not such an ignorant innocent. He was right to have come, although he shouldn't have walked. He hadn't arrived in very good condition. But he was here and he would wait. Harold bent over and with exquisite pleasure, took his shoes off. He leaned back deep into the chair and closed his dry and stinging eyelids. In a little while, surely, the coolness would get through the skin, where it was making him shiver, and in toward his bones.

She didn't make any noise, returning, but he felt her presence, opened his eyes and struggled more erect to take the glass, and the paper napkin upon which she was holding it, into both his hands. He drank thirstily and thanked her with all his heart.

She smiled, just a trifle falsely, and sat down on the ottoman again. Her eyes seemed solemn, and he had revived enough to feel a little awkward with a stranger. He put the glass on the table and played with the paper napkin. It was white, with a name printed in a mahogany brown script across one corner. THE WHITMANS. "I used to be so impressed, you know," he said shyly. "Just think, people who had their name printed on their paper napkins."

She said, with faint impatience, "Everybody does. Tell me, why did you *walk?* You said, all the way? But that must be about seventy-five miles!"

"Not counting up and down, either." He smiled at her. "Oh, I was kind of lured into it, I guess. I

11

started out, walking to the bus. But it was so great, you know, walking and looking around. I thought, why should I settle for a stinky bus? I had it in my mind to hitch-hike, maybe. By the time, I was out on the highway I found out that's not so easy anymore. Anyhow, I got to thinking, they might ask me where I'd come from. . . . Maybe they'd be scared."

He hadn't really tried to hitch a ride. Walking was a wonderful way to get to thinking, alone and free.

"You were released from there on Monday?" the girl was saying, in her brisk tone.

He hesitated. He really was too tired to explain the whole thing. "Well . . . I didn't start walking until Tuesday morning," he told her. "I have a room in the town. School doesn't start for a while yet. I wanted to find out . . . Maybe you can tell me. Where is the baby?"

He didn't know whether he was a coward or not, to ask *her*. She wasn't answering. Her eyes opened very wide and she looked perfectly astonished. "But don't you *know!*"

How would I know? he thought. Who would tell me? And why don't you know that I wouldn't know? Don't you know that I was cast out and thrown away? But he spoke patiently. "I've written letters. Nobody answered. I *said* that I was leaving the hospital, on Monday. I was afraid they might have moved away."

"Didn't Myra tell you?" the girl said, with strange urgency. She was watching him, most intently.

"Do you mean *she* wrote to me?" He couldn't understand the question. "I didn't get *any* letters," he

12

explained. The girl frowned, and he went on, still patient. "I've got no folks and my buddies aren't the writing kind. All I had were a couple of legal notices. One, that the divorce was final. I guess that gave me the nerve . . ." His voice was going dreary again. He thought he knew what the trouble was. "You can tell me," he said gently, "if the baby died."

The girl sat straight with a jolt. "Oh, no, no, no! He's all right. Oh, I'm sorry. I was thinking of something else. He's in a special school, that's all. The Patterson School for deaf children. It's about forty miles north of here on the coast road—"

"I know where that is," he cut in joyously. "I see. That's *good*."

"You did know that he was born deaf!" The girl's voice was careful. It promised kindness, but not too much kindness. She was paying attention, that was the thing. She was really listening.

"Oh, yes. Oh, yes. They let me hold him, once." He could remember the feel of the little soft light body. "I was the one who noticed. It's a thing about the formation of the ear. My father had it and my brother, who died. But not Mom or me. I told Wendy about the risk, but she said she didn't care."

No, Wendy didn't care in those days. Wendy, so wild and wonderful, didn't care for anything.

"And I believed her," he murmured, and glanced up, somberly.

"They'll teach him to talk, you know," the girl said heartily, as if to raise his spirits. "And they may even be able to invent some kind of hearing aid."

13

"That's wonderful, isn't it?" But he kept somber. "Wendy must be . . . ." He looked behind him, and up the long curve of the stairs, to where the wrought iron of the stair-rail continued across the balcony of the second story. "I suppose Wendy is living—near him?"

She said, "No," throwing the syllable away, and the corner of her mouth twitched.

Their eyes met and there was a telepathic flash. He knew that he and she were the same kind of people. She, too, would suppose that a mother would wish to be near her child. She must have been brought up to assume this, as Harold had been. His family hadn't been rich, as the Whitmans were, but it had been a family; it had assumed such things. Over and above his personal loss, it was too bad that he was the only one left now, from such a family, because four people, who looked out for each other without having to think about it, made something better than just four people. He was convinced that this girl knew what he was thinking and agreed with him.

But she plunged into more questions. (The baby was all right. It wasn't that, then. Yet, something was bothering her.) "You didn't walk night and day, did you? Have you got any money? Where did you sleep?"

"I haven't much money right now," he answered. "Enough for snacks. That's all right. I thought Mr. Whitman might lend me a part of the bus fare back, since I have some expectations. Not that I came to ask *them* for anything, except where the baby is. I feel . . . I felt very strongly that I ought to know that."

What he was saying came back oddly to his own ears. It was true enough, but not enough of the truth.

"I wish you had telephoned," she said, and bit her lips.

"Yes, but the truth is, I came myself—" he struggled to express the whole truth—"because I'm still . . . and I don't want to be, but I *am still* . . . afraid of these people."

And that's as close as I can get, he thought. I have to speak to them and hear them answer. I have to look at them and meet their eyes.

"Where did you spend last night?" she was demanding.

"Last night? I slept on a lawn swing. The house looked empty. There was a big dog, but he was friendly. In fact, he kept me company. I was glad to have him." He thought it was small talk. He smiled.

"Where was this?" She wasn't smiling.

"A little town . . ." He couldn't remember the name.

"Did anybody see you? Did you talk with anyone? Last night? Or this morning?"

He moved his head, wonderingly. "I started early, this morning, because I was cold. What's the matter?"

Now he knew that she had been gathering toward a resolution. Her face changed. She sprang up on her good lithe legs. "You shouldn't have come here and you've got to leave," she said decisively. She was a brisk crisp kind of girl, with lots of energy. "Right now. You had better get on a bus as quick

15

as you can and get out of this town. *I'll* give you some money."

He twisted in the chair to watch her. She ran to the stairs, which began at the edge of the big window, and swiftly up the first short flight to the landing, which made a curving balcony upon the curving wall. She opened the wooden door, ornately carved to make a decoration here, into the turret room. It was a bedroom, he knew that, used for a guest room, for overflow or unimportant guests. It was halfway up and halfway down, and it was round, which is a very unhandy shape, he remembered someone saying. It had a tiny bathroom, put in as an afterthought, which cut up the space grotesquely, built as square as could be against the rounding outer wall, in which the windows were too small for so large a room. He had glanced in, he remembered, when one of the maids had been cleaning one morning. He remembered the strange green gloom where the eastern light came feebly through the leaves of the big tree.

He was shivering again. He stood up, slowly, and as his weight came upon his feet he knew that the left one was a normally tired foot, but the right one, which had once been broken, was more seriously damaged. He limped toward the stairs.

The girl flashed out of the turret room and stood above him on the balcony, a flat black purse in both hands. She began to rummage in it. "Oh nuts! I should have cashed a traveler's check yesterday. Never mind. There's some change, at least. Or I could meet you . . . No, that's too risky."

She seemed to be talking to herself. He said,

16

"What's wrong?"

She took a step to look straight down into his face. "*You* weren't in this house last night." She announced this.

Of course not, he thought. Of course not. "No," he said.

"Then I don't see why you should walk right into it, now."

She started down but he stopped her. "Now, wait. I've come all this way—"

"To find out where the baby is? Well, I've told you."

Standing on his left foot, feeling dizzy, Harold began to shake his head. "That wasn't all."

"You don't know a thing about it, do you?" the girl said softly, with compassion in her voice. "I didn't think you would. Oh please, just get away."

"From what?" he said severely.

She took a deep breath and made a grimace. "Well, you've walked right in. Listen, you are supposed to be one of those berserk ex-husbands." She was still on the stairs, looking down. "The police are looking for you," she said, as if it broke her heart to tell him so.

Harold steadied himself. "Why?"

She ran down and came close to him. She put her hand on his arm and he had to struggle not to lean, not to fall. Her gray eyes were very clear and sad, but her voice was still brisk. "Because somebody got in here last night and beat up Myra Whitman, your ex . . . step . . . whatever-she-was mother-in-law. And she is in a coma in the hospital, *here*. That's where I thought you'd come from, at first.

17

That's where they all *are*. And Cousin Ted is fit to be tied. He is even . . ." She sucked in her breath. Her hand was strong, now, on his arm. He must be leaning. "I don't see how you ever got through," she said, in a worried tone. "Maybe that coat. Why are you wearing a white coat?" She was trying to lead him to the chair.

"My orderly's coat," he said. "To be clean." He moved out of her grasp, stumbling. He put up his hands and caught hold of the iron balusters. With his back to her, trying to understand the full import of the situation and already understanding it too well, he asked her, "Why do they think *I* beat up Myra?"

She answered with a quiet respect, very clearly, "Because you beat up Wendy once. Because you've been in a mental hospital. Because you wrote that you were leaving there on Monday. Because the divorce is final and you didn't want the divorce. You just . . . fit the pattern, I suppose."

He didn't look around. "Is that all?"

This time she did not answer.

So he turned. He made himself able to stand up. "Where is Wendy?"

"She . . . she still lives here."

"I see." He swayed. "So it's going to happen all over again."

She caught his arm again and held it, strongly. With her other hand she touched his neck, under the ear. "Are you feverish?"

"I don't know. What did Wendy say?"

"Wendy said she saw you running down the drive last night."

18

Well, there it was. It was so wrong as to be some-how right. He almost laughed.

After a while, he was in the chair again and the girl was on the ottoman, watching him anxiously. He had the sense that she had gone to look out the front door, that nobody was coming, that they were here, in this cool and somehow sunken room, safe and alone, for a little while more. Before it happened to him, all over again.

He said calmly, speculatively, "Why does she tell these lies? Why do they always believe her? I understand myself much better now. I had to learn. But I don't understand these people."

"What did they do to you? I've always wondered." Her face was close to his, her skin was very fair. Something about her eyelids kept a secret. "I learned some time ago to watch out for Wendy. Tell me?"

He might as well tell her while there was time. "I didn't ever beat up Wendy. Ever. It's true I didn't want the divorce, because I wanted to make a family." (A family that would be a family, as he understood a family should be.) "Out of Wendy and me and the baby," he went on. "Of course, I was in the service then. I couldn't send much money." (But he would have worked. He would have made a family and a home.) "But when they wanted me to, well, stand still for Wendy to sue me. . . . You know how it's done. The man has to play that he's guilty. I said, No, I *wasn't.* And I *wouldn't.* So that's when I had to watch her bruise her own arms and

19

claw her own face—because when I tried to stop her, that was worse. Well, so she got the divorce and the baby, too. There wasn't a way . . . not a way in the world. How could I call Wendy Whitman a liar, with her folks behind her? *I* had no folks. I was nineteen years old. She wouldn't have had to do that. She wanted to be rid of me, she could have been. Without telling such a lie and taking everything . . . you know . . . everything away from me." There was no whine in his voice, he was just telling her.

The girl said, "And you *saw* her?"

"In a dream, you wonder?" He sat up straighter. "Well, you see, I have *been* analyzed. Oh, I've had hypnosis, drugs. They tried the whole works on me. Oh, they tried, in the worst way, to find some part of me that 'knew' I'd done it. But there wasn't any. I was a strange case, I guess. I'd actually been frustrated. And here I go again."

He smiled at the perfection of the wrongness of it. He smiled at the girl, who was looking troubled. "At least I'll know better, this time, than to hold it all in," he told her, "until I'm fighting like a wildcat whenever anybody looks cross-eyed at me. That's how I broke my foot, back in camp, after she started the divorce. And I fought the doctors and the nurses, too. They finally sent me to psychiatry."

"And to that hospital, for all this time?" she said delicately.

He knew she wanted to believe him. "Would you like to call them?" he said, gently. "Then you'd *know* that I was discharged as a patient months ago. As soon as they got it out of me what had happened, and that it was true. I cried for about a week, but I stopped hitting people. But, see, my foot's no good for the army. I had nowhere and nobody. There was just this old great-uncle, who died. I had a notice—"

"There's no time, now," she interrupted.

But he wanted to tell her a little more. "I'm going to *be* a doctor, I hope. They let me work there. I got fascinated. Now I want the training. Dr. Wesley says I can do it. I'm starting school . . . I mean, I *was*."

He looked around. The good dream faded. No, first, it was going to happen to him all over again.

She was tugging at his arm to get him to his feet. "Oh, hurry, please, before they come. Just go away."

"Is there any use in that?" he asked her delicately, not wishing to offend. He felt dizzy standing, and his head was very light.

"Please believe me. You can't be found in this house. Or in this town, even. Maybe it doesn't have to happen to you all over again."

"How come you believe what I say, miss?" Harold had begun to wonder.

"Edie," she said, fiercely. "I'm Edie. Oh, listen, I lived here myself when I was a teen-ager and *I* knew little Wendy."

He wasn't taking it in. "I'm glad if you do believe me, but I can't see why." Isn't she a member of this family, he was thinking.

"Then I'll tell you something," said Edie. "I came here for a couple of weeks between jobs, just for my own sake to . . . to see . . ."

21

There was that telepathic flash again. "To see," said Harold slowly, "whether you could, somehow, for your own sake . . . now, manage to stand up to them? Or even—forgive them?"

"I suppose that's it," she said impatiently, but with friendliness, too. "That's something like it. Do you know that you are burning? How are you going to make it to the bus? I wish I had a car."

"I'll have to stand up to them," he said remotely.

"No, not now. I'll tell you what." She was turning him and guiding him. "Both maids are away. There's only Mrs. Beck, and she's busy. Nobody will go into the turret room but me. Please, wait in there. Will you, please? Just let me pave the way for you. Let me break it to them gently that you've come."

"Why?" he said, stubborn, knowing that she hadn't told him everything.

"All right." She took the challenge. "Because Cousin Ted has cast himself in the role of the heroic defender of his womenfolk and he's got a loaded gun in his pocket and he is stupid enough to shoot you. Is there any sense in that?"

He blinked at her. "Well, not for *me,*" he said, half-humorously. He knew she believed what she had said. He was inclined to believe it too.

So he went up the stone stairs in his stocking feet, one hand on the rail, her strong hand under his other arm. He was very dizzy. He said, "But I don't know why *you* believe me."

"Myra's had her hair dyed red, for a year."

"What?"

"Don't argue," Edie said. "You don't feel well

enough to figure that out. You don't feel well enough to be shot at, either." She turned him into the turret room and shut the door behind them.

Chapter Two

There was one thing about the turret room. Once you had closed the small, but heavy, wooden door, you felt sheltered. The door was thick, the walls were thick. The room was cool. Between the ceiling and the beating California sun, there was an attic, a tiled roof, and the heavy shadow of the tree.

Edie Thompson made the boy stretch out on the double bed. She found some aspirin in the medicine cabinet and made him take it. There was a flowered quilt, kept folded at the foot of the bed. She pulled it over his ankles for the sake of the sense of shelter it would add. All the while, she spoke soothingly. She would talk to the Whitmans. She would fend for him. She would try to make them see that they were mistaken, or at least that they might be mistaken, before the sight of him could shock them into doing something foolish. It made more sense, she said. And he needed rest.

He rested quietly. He was a good-looking boy. Naturally, thought Edie. Wendy would never have taken up with anyone who wasn't. He was medium tall, on the slim side, brown-haired, brown-eyed, and his face was saved from prettiness by some rugged carving of his long thin nose. But a boy, very young—maybe a country boy. Just an ordinary nice kid, a little naïve. One without defenses, who had suffered in a way that the tougher kind of young male animal, the city kids, the gang kids (whom Edie knew), might not. She had worked with some of *them*, the very young ones. Of course, he was running a fever. Maybe that made him seem in need. Gave him his air of helplessness. She wanted to help him.

Edie was a social worker and she knew better than to call her judgment infallible or her belief the guarantee of truth. But after all, she had been conducting interviews, for a year and a half now, in the grubbiest sections of a great city, and she thought her chances were fair to spot a phony, a loony, or a criminal. Edie was a girl with firm opinions, and a good deal of self-confidence these days. She was energetic and sometimes impatient with people who were not. This was a bit of handicap in her profession. Sometimes Edie was not altogether sure that she had chosen the right profession, but its practice had given her some skills. A kind of intuition, for instance, based on experience.

If this boy was what the newspapers call "berserk," she would be very much surprised. She thought he was, if anything, too innocently sentimental. She could not sense in him the devious cleverness he would have to have to toss out that mention of Myra's coloring—*if* he had quarreled with a redheaded Myra here, last night. "Berserk" people were not clever. It was a contradiction. Of course, he might have two personalities. It could be Jekyll lying there, weary and gentle and sad. Hyde

25

could have burst in last night. She didn't believe that. She believed what he had told her—all of it.

The fact was, she didn't believe *Wendy*.

Edie had moved to one of the narrow windows and was looking down at the driveway and the gates. They would be back soon. Then she must be the go-between. That was it. Be a buffer. Try to steady the situation. There was a certain amount of hysteria in it. Assumptions had been made. The Whitmans were perfectly convinced that Harold Page had done it. Edie must try to crack open their minds and insert enough doubt so that the poor kid might not be hurt too much. Not again.

There was that. She thought, *If* what he says is true (and I believe him), then he is tender to unjust suspicions. For him it opens an old wound, it hurts more. Oh, there was some physical danger. If the boy had been greeted by Cousin Ted in that gentleman's present agitated state, Edie thought it quite possible that Cousin Ted would have shot, at least *at* him. But there are worse wounds than a bullet makes.

Edie leaned on the wall and felt power curling her fingers. She was the go-between. She knew both sides. She had lived here herself and knew the regime. She had been brought up in a frugal household, however, by parents both loving and high-minded, and she had seen the seamy side besides, in her work. It seemed to Edie that the duty fell upon her with a click of fitness, and she accepted it, not without joy. It was a joy for which she had thirsted, and had not found yet. Maybe her new job . . . with a heavier load, more cases.

Maybe. Meanwhile, she believed in Harold Page, and her joy was the joy of battle. She would fight for him.

Edie had a dim notion that somewhere along the line she was merrily rationalizing. But didn't everyone? She believed him when he said that Wendy had cheated and lied. That much was easy. Did she believe that he had walked so far?

Yes, she believed that too. For one thing, it was too fantastic not to be true. Truth was the most fantastic thing in the world. Sometimes she thought that people knocked themselves out, split their human brains, trying to make order in a world that was *really* and incorrigibly fantastic. He said he had walked seventy-five miles. It was possible. Human beings *could* walk, the motorcar notwithstanding. And there was his fatigue, his limp . . . *his shoes!*

She saw a car turn into the drive and after it, another, and yet another. *Three* carloads of people arriving? Fantastic—But what about his shoes?

She went swiftly to the door. The boy did not stir. Edie shut him in, alone, and ran down the lower flight of the stairs. The dusty empty pathetic shoes were near the chair. Edie made a swipe across the carpet with her foot and swept them under the chair as the outer door opened, and she heard Cousin Ted's voice.

He had a high voice with an irritating nasal quality. "I want to talk to Charles, Mother, and these other people."

"All right, Ted. All right. All right," said old Mrs. Whitman. She entered and the house became her house, the kingdom was her kingdom.

27

She was a spry little woman of seventy-five, dressed elegantly, if uncomfortably for the hot day, in a gray silk suit, a costume complete with small flowered hat, with gloves, with neat gray shoes. She came nimbly down into the big room and did not greet, but waited to be greeted.

"Hi, Granny," said Edie, feeling her heart give a great guilty leap. "How is Myra?"

Granny began to chatter in her clear, light, well-articulated manner. "Oh, mercy! Oh, my! I am very sorry that I went." She proceeded to the sofa and seated herself with good control, without, in any way, collapsing. "Myra is just lying there, looking a perfect fright, by the way. I can't help thinking it was rude to go and stare at her. Especially since her mouth is open." The old lady began to remove her gloves, and Edie, watching her, felt the same old bewilderment. She never had been able to tell whether Granny meant to be funny, meant to be tart, or simply meant what she said.

"But what does the doctor say?" she asked.

"Oh, *he* is very calm about the whole thing, the doctor is. They are making tests. Maybe they'll operate. Maybe, mind you. Or, as far as I can understand it, maybe Myra will simply open her eyes and come to." Granny removed her hat.

"Then she can tell us what happened, I suppose," said Edie with a sense of solution.

"You can suppose all you like, Edie, my dear," said Granny, "but it seems that a blow on the head joggles the cells or whatever is *in* there . . ."

"Oh?"

"And if Myra doesn't remember, that will seem

odd, don't you think?" said old Mrs. Whitman, putting her white head to one side. She had blue eyes that somehow never seemed connected with what Granny was saying. The eyes kept moving, as if something very wary hid inside and did not much care what was being said or done, but watched out for itself. "Suppose one were minding one's own business and woke up in a hospital, two or three days later, people having been staring . . ."

But Edie had caught sight of the water glass, in the corner of her eye. It seemed to shine like a star. Without thought, her mind occupied with dismay at the idea that Myra might never remember, and guilt for her own equivocal position, Edie moved out of the range of Granny's eyes, snatched up the glass from which Harold Page had drunk, and slipped away to the far end of the high mantelpiece, where she tucked the glass behind an ornament.

"I do hope," Granny was saying, "that it never happens to me. Where are you? Where is Mrs. Beck? I want a cup of tea. Ted had to go and see those grubby people and haul me about with him. I don't know what possessed me. I had presumed that I had reached a stage of life . . . Edie?"

"I'm here," said Edie. Her heart was racing. I have got to get over this panicking, she thought. What I propose to do, I had better do well. And soon. I had better consider how I am going to talk to Granny.

". . . when I need not be troubled," Granny rippled on, "by any miserable notions of duty. For pity's sake, doesn't one reach a point when one has *done* it? *Iced* tea, I think."

29

Edie said, soothingly, "Mrs. Beck is lying down. She had such a bad night—"

"So did we all," Granny cut in. "Ambulance, commotion, police. It was quite stimulating."

And again, Edie was not sure whether this was supposed to be sarcastic or just fact.

This old lady was not really Edie's grandmother. She was her great-aunt. Edie had fallen into the way of calling her Granny (Wendy did) when she had lived here, seven or eight years ago. At that time Granny had been Authority, whimsical and powerful, and naturally resented. Now Edith Thompson was a person who had been in the world, and Lila Whitman had no real authority over her. But somehow, she was just as powerful and just as whimsical as ever.

Edie sat down on the edge of the sofa, beside her, and said earnestly, "Granny, did you hear *anything* last night, when it happened?"

Granny's dainty claw fumbled with the tiny box she wore on her breast. "I never hear anything at night, Edie, for the simple reason that I cannot sleep upon my hearing aid. One of these days *I'll* wake up and find I've been hit on the head by some madman . . . or whatever he did to poor Myra."

"They think," Edie began to recapitulate, "there was some kind of struggle and she fell. . . ."

But Granny had half risen from the sofa. She seemed to be staring across the room.

"What?" gasped Edie. (What have I forgotten? What does she see? Does she know he is here?)

But the old lady sank back. "Oh, mercy! I suppose it *is* a mercy, they left no X to mark the spot."

Myra had struck her head, the theory was, on the hard tile of the hearth.

Edie began to think that the old lady might be enjoying herself. "Do you *believe* it was Harold Page?" she said, a trifle angrily.

"Of course it was," said Granny. "Oh, he has been such a nuisance! I could have told Wendy, in the beginning. She didn't ask me. Well, I keep quiet, you know."

No, you don't, thought Edie.

"One may as well," Granny ran on. "One might better. Wendy never listens. Few do. Few do."

"Granny, will you please listen to me for a minute?"

But old Mrs. Whitman had no intention of listening very much. She was off. "There was Wendy," she explained, "all of sixteen long years old but barely. And 'everybody' was getting married."

Oh surely, thought Edie, listening hard, that is sarcasm. A form of—what? Humor?

"By 'everybody,' " Granny continued, "we must understand, first, her father (to Myra, of course) and second, one girl in Wendy's class who had eloped, which exploit was regarded with a certain enviable awe. So Wendy picked up this soldier. Of all things! Ted ought to have had it annulled right away. But Ted indulges Wendy scandalously, if you ask me. Which he does not. Since Genevieve died, he has had some notion that Wendy *cannot* be crossed. To him, it is like speaking ill of the dead." Granny sighed. "I don't suppose," she said and her blue eyes wagged in their sockets, "that my son has ever been the most brilliant boy in the world. Not

31

that it matters."

Edie opened her mouth but before she could speak, Granny smoothed at her skirt briskly and said, "We have plenty of money."

I never will understand her, thought Edie. "How can you be so sure that it was Harold Page?" she said, coldly.

"Oh, for pity's sake, *of course* it was Harold Page. Wendy saw him." Granny continued to brush her skirt.

"Couldn't Wendy ever be mistaken? Like any other human being?" said Edie, rather hotly. "Even so, she doesn't say she saw him inside the house. The police didn't find any fingerprints."

"Oh, Edie," said Granny, not bothering to lift her eyelids, "don't be so retarded. Nobody leaves fingerprints anymore. Passé. Passé."

And there it was again, the puzzle. Was the old lady being funny?

"And obviously," said Granny, "he *was* inside the house, because, if not, he couldn't have done it."

Mrs. Beck, the housekeeper, from where she was standing, just within the dining room, could hear the voices in the big room. Neither voice was the one she always listened for. She smoothed her clean white silk uniform and stepped forward. It was time she made an appearance.

She said, politely, "Do you need me, Mrs. Whitman? How is Miss Myra, ma'am?"

The old lady turned her frosty head and spoke in the way she had that was always so cool, and a

32

little bit nasty. "She'll be all right—sooner or later and more or less, that is. May I have some iced tea, please, Mrs. Beck?"

At least she always says "please," Mrs. Beck thought, with satisfaction. "Yes, ma'am," she said in the humble, but cool, way she had long ago adopted. "Miss Edith?"

The cousin, or whatever she was, who was here for the fortnight, said, "No, thank you." Then the girl's gaze flicked toward the stairs. "Wait. Yes, I will, thank you."

Mrs. Beck looked toward the stairs, herself. "Is Miss Wendy here?" she cooed. She never could help that change in her voice.

"No, no," said the old lady. "What's his name— Ronnie Mungo—came and fetched her at the hospital. Otherwise she wouldn't have gone, I imagine."

Mrs. Beck said nothing. Let the old lady be aware that Wendy didn't care for Myra. Anyone could know that.

"He carried her off to the country club for lunch. Why not? With plenty of lemon."

Mrs. Beck made the submissive duck of her head that she had long ago adopted. Go make the iced tea, then. Mrs. Beck had some powdered tea. Good enough, with water from the tap. She went through the long dining room and turned the corner to the kitchen.

Mrs. Beck was fifty years old. She was tall and there wasn't much flesh on her big bones. She had been in this house a long time. It was her kingdom. She had come when the first Mrs. Theodore Whitman was still alive, Miss Genevieve, who had died

33

before the year was out. After that, it hadn't taken long to shake the house into the pattern that Mrs. Beck desired. She and the old lady had an unwritten compact. The old lady got whatever she wanted, and Mrs. Beck ran the house. When Miss Myra had come along, Mrs. Beck had been leery of *her*, for a while, and taken protective measures. But it had turned out that Miss Myra, the second wife, the one whose age fell between the old lady and little Wendy, had known better than to try to interfere in any way. She had never tried to run the house. She had never tried to run anybody. She had kept herself to herself and minded her own business — until last night.

Mrs. Beck knew how Myra was. She had called the hospital, herself, and inquired. Myra was in a coma. Mrs. Beck turned on the water with a twist of her strong wrist to let it run cold.

In the big room Edie was saying, "Granny, when I was eighteen you wouldn't let *me* have a date with Ronnie Mungo."

She hadn't meant to say that, but it was an old sore point, and now that Edie was grown and out from under authority she could discuss it, couldn't she? She could find out for sure. The old lady's face, however, showed no concern, no ruffling, not even the memory.

"I wouldn't?" she said placidly. "Why was that, I wonder? Well, Wendy will marry him, I suppose — or so she said on Sunday. Now that she's legally free. And they will go and travel about and be gay

34

with their money, which will suit them very well."

She doesn't care, thought Edie. She simply does not care. "Tell me this," Edie said, wishing she could take hold of the narrow, elegant shoulders and shake—hard, "Why on earth would Harold Page get into this house and fight with *Myra?*"

"Myra," said Granny, with a thoughtful air, "can be *very* annoying, in her quiet little way . . ."

Edie was tired of trying to guess whether this was in fun or not. "Would you answer me?"

"For pity's sake," said Granny, "what is Harold Page to you, child? Or he to Hecuba? A madman needn't have a reason."

"It's pretty passé to say 'madman,' Granny."

"I beg your pardon."

"Mad? *Just* mad?" If this is a quarrel, thought Edie, then let's have it.

"But of course he is," said the old lady carelessly. "He must be mad to do such a thing. Myra may be annoying at times, but one shouldn't knock her on the head. One can always manage to be *more* annoying, or something of the sort. That is, if one is sane."

Edie strangled incredulous laughter. "He did it because he is mad? He must be mad because he did it?" she asked.

"Well?"

"But that's circular!" Edie threw out her hands. Maybe Granny was simply rather stupid. Maybe that was the answer to the riddle of Granny.

The old lady was as slippery as water. She said tartly, "Nothing of the sort. Or, if so, what about it? It happens to be what happened *and* what usually does."

Edie swallowed.

"Still . . ." said Granny, "I wish her mouth had *not* been open." Her own old lips came tight together and seemed to knead each other.

Chapter Three

Edith Thompson was an orphan. She had come here, badly shaken by the sudden death of both her parents, when she had just turned seventeen years old. She had been given board and room, here. She had gone to high school in this town. Wendy was not at public school, but attended Miss Somebody-or-other's. Public school, however, was good enough for Edith Thompson.

She had not made many friends in high school. Girls who lived as frugally as she had lived were shy of the Whitman ménage. Girls who lived as the Whitmans lived were few and not very friendly. Boys were much the same. In this house, Edie had been a poor relation, taken in physically but in no other way. Her cousin Wendy had been eleven, and twelve, and never her companion. On the contrary! Edie had been miserable and lonely. But after she had won through the period of lonely mourning, her native energy had seethed. She would get away. *She* would get away.

At eighteen, then, she had quietly enrolled herself in a college, far away, back East, and paid her first semester's tuition from her own small hoard. And bought her ticket. When the time came, she had quietly packed her clothing and gone. It was true that old Mrs. Whitman had then given her a check which rebuilt the little emergency fund, but Edie had worked and scrounged the first year, won a scholarship the next year, and after that it had been easier. When she took her first full-time job, she had sent the money back, with a letter that tried to say how valuable the security had been to her. She'd had a letter in reply that had said almost nothing.

Edie had prepared herself for social work because that had been her parents' field, and she had been taught to think that it was important and fulfilling. She had now served her apprenticeship and was going into a "better" job. Sometimes Edie suspected that she'd been kicked upstairs. She didn't have her father's patience, but a temper of her own. It was hard for her to resign herself to things-as-they-are. Edie tended to try to push things, and people, around to change, to progress, to *do* something about something. Well, the new job paid more and there would at least be more of a kind of responsibility. Whether it was the right kind for her, Edie did not yet know.

There was a two weeks' interval of leisure, however, and she had written.

Edie wasn't sure just why. The Whitmans were her only relatives. That served for a surface reason. But there is such a thing as wishing to knit up the several threads of your past, especially in a period of transition. She had wanted to come again, on a different basis. She had wanted to see, with older eyes, the scenes of her youth. To taste, with a more mellow palate, that which had been once so bitter.

She had written and Granny had answered "Do come," and added, "if you like," seasoning cordiality with a touch of indifference.

When Edie had arrived, late on Sunday last, it was just as if she had never gone away at all, or at least as if she had not been doing anything in the meantime. The Whitmans made no effort to entertain her. They seemed to assume that they were taking her in, giving her board and room because she was poor and she needed these, just as they had before.

They did not ask about her work. When she told them what it was, Granny had said, "Edie, you do remind me of your mother. Going around the world, doing good. A nosy busybodying and presumptuous kind of career that never attracted anyone else in the family. I can't imagine why it ever attracted her."

She fell in love with my father, Edie had answered, but not aloud. She felt that Granny could not imagine *that*.

Edie took note of what had happened here in the meantime. Genevieve gone; Myra, instead. But Myra had made no effort to form an independent judgment of Edith Thompson. Courteous and aloof, she treated Edie like a poor relation. Myra was a small-boned, sleek little person, not as young as she used to be but much younger than her husband. She moved quietly from one social engagement to another and spent the Whitman money with shrewd good taste. One day, Edie guessed,

39

when Granny was gone, Myra would enter into her kingdom.

Wendy—to whom so much seemed to have happened in the meantime, marriage, childbirth, divorce, and now an engagement to marry again—Wendy was still in no way a companion. She went in and out. She went by. She scarcely seemed to notice her cousin Edie. Of course, she was only just nineteen years old and naturally intent upon her own affairs. Wendy was going to marry Ronnie Mungo.

And that was that.

After the first day, Edie had shrugged her shoulders and sallied forth to sample the climate and observe the customs of the natives in southern California. She had prowled the bright little town, gone to the bright beach, ferreted out a concert to which she had gone, alone, on Wednesday night. And come back into the middle of the commotion, just as the ambulance was pulling away.

She had tried to be steady and helpful. But Wendy, up in her room, did not need her. She had Mrs. Beck. Granny refused to budge from the center of things. Nobody could put her to bed, with assorted comforts. Edie had tried to help with breakfast this morning, but Mrs. Beck was there in the kitchen and not in need of her.

When the Whitmans had gone off to the hospital, late this morning, Edie had stayed behind. She did not belong to this household. She did not need them, either, and she was fully resolved not to stay the whole two weeks, where she had no place.

But now she had made herself a place, indeed—

right in the middle. She had hidden Harold Page in the turret room and she had promised to do something to help him. She had better get on with it. But how?

There was no reasoning with Granny.

Edie had seen three cars turn in at the gates. She knew that there were people around and about. Even so, she was startled when the front door burst open and three men marched in.

Cousin Ted came first. He was in his fifties, a dapper man of middle height, with a torso too bulky for the rest of him. He seemed to dwindle toward the floor and his very small feet. Dark-rimmed glasses rode on his smooth pink face and his hair, still dark, was like a cap that he wore pushed well back from his high rounded forehead. He was in a state of dramatic excitement, as if this were his kingdom and he were in command.

He rushed to the foot of the stairs and made an ushering sweep of his arm. "Start up there, please. My daughter's room and one other."

"Yes, sir," said the second man.

Edie was on her feet, her heart in her throat. The second man was a perfect stranger, stocky in a blue suit, obedient to Cousin Ted. He put his wide black shoes on the treads. Edie's feet in their black slippers whirled her to the newel post. "What is he *doing,* Cousin Ted?" Edie sagged, inside, as the blue back simply crossed the balcony above and went on up.

"He is closing and fastening all the shutters on this house," said Cousin Ted, giving her a fierce and hostile glance.

"Mercy!" said Granny. "Isn't that going to be rather dismal, Ted?"

"Oh, Mother . . ." Cousin Ted had a way of saying this, on the puff of a sigh, whenever his mother deflated him.

"Good afternoon, Charles," piped Granny.

The third man had come in less precipitously than the others. He stood beside the big window with his hands in his pockets, looking at nothing. He was a heavy man with a strong-featured face and cold blue eyes. He made a perfunctory murmur of names. "Mrs. Whitman. Miss Edith."

"Mr. Tyler," said Edie. She had met him last night.

She was thinking of Harold Page. If they were to burst in on him now, with no warning to either side. *No!* Edie rounded the newel-post and began to slip up the stairs herself. "Cousin Ted," she said, "there *are* no shutters on the turret room."

"I am very well aware of that, Edie, since this happens to be the house where I was born." Cousin Ted was testy.

Charles Tyler had stepped close to the glass and was looking out and upward to the right. Edie was not sure that she wasn't going to faint, poised there on the fourth step, because if Harold Page, for any reason, happened to be standing in the window on that side . . . But Tyler said, without much interest, "Tree looks like a way to get in, all right."

"I know that, too," snapped Cousin Ted. "That's why one of the guards is going to watch that tree."

"Guards?" gasped Edie "Do you mean—policemen?"

"No, no," said Cousin Ted, who, in the role of the forceful man, was managing to be extremely cross. "I've hired professionals who will do as *I* say. One for each corner, at the back of the house. The solarium is vulnerable. So is the kitchen and the cellar door. But nobody will break in here a second time."

This proclamation rang on the air. Cousin Ted pulled in his chin and, for a moment, looked fat and satisfied.

Edie said, "But I thought . . . Nobody *broke* in. You didn't think so last night, sir?" She was speaking to Charles Tyler, who was the Chief of Police in this town.

He tilted his face to look at her. "Myra may have let him in. After all, she knew him."

"She should have known better," chirped Granny. "*I* wouldn't have let him in."

"Don't be alarmed," Tyler said to her with a kind of professional comforting, "I have prowl cars in the whole area. They'll find him."

Cousin Ted seemed to take offense. "And how a prowl car is going to find an escaped madman who is more likely to be hiding in the shrubbery than walking along the street . . ."

Tyler's cold eye brushed over him. "We know our business."

Mrs. Beck came in with a tray upon which she carried two tall glasses with lemon slices perched upon their rims. There was a hospitable shuffle and murmur, below, to which Edie paid no attention, because she could see the man in the blue suit, the guard or whoever he was, starting down. She herself had reached the balcony and now she put her back against the door to the turret room. If necessary, she would say, "Don't come in here. I have something to tell you, first." But what would she say, next?

Cousin Ted called out, "Conrad? You didn't forget the window at the end of the hall?"

"No, sir," the man called downward. "We can have pretty tight security, I'd say, Mr. Whitman." He was descending. "Where now?" He paused just one step above where Edie stood. He had his hand on the banister and his coat fell open.

Edie said, in quick desperation, loudly, "Mr. Tyler, this man is wearing a gun. Is that all right?"

"Certainly he has a gun," said Cousin Ted furiously. "How else can he protect us?"

"And Cousin Ted has a gun *too*," cried Edie. "What if they shoot the wrong person? *I* think it's terribly dangerous."

Granny made one of her remarks that was either silly panic or brave comedy. "I shall turn off my hearing aid. I cannot *abide* the noise of guns." Then she took the tea.

But Tyler had lifted his heavy head. "You've got three qualified men for this job, Conrad?"

"Yes, sir." The man in the blue suit was intent upon proving his answer. He came down the one step, he crossed the balcony, where Edie was shrinking against her door, he thumped his wide feet on the lower treads. The wood of the door at her back was solid and opaque and she let it hold her up.

Tyler and the man exchanged a few low sentences, with the effect of using an inside language, unintel-

44

ligible to the ordinary public. Then Tyler turned on Cousin Ted, who stood there, goggling. "You'd better not carry a gun, Ted." The Chief's choice of words was milder than his tone.

"I tell you, Charles, if this escaped madman shows himself on my property, I have the right . . ."

Tyler said, brushing him off again, "Not you. Trained people. Put it away."

So Edie thought she saw her solution. Trained people, of course. It was Charles Tyler to whom she must appeal, just as soon as Cousin Ted, who really was a stupid man, had put away his gun. Or perhaps she could manage to speak to Mr. Tyler alone, and that would be even better. She perceived that Mrs. Beck was standing, stranded, with the other glass of iced tea on the tray. Edie did not want to move away from the turret room door. Not yet. So she said, "Put it on the table, please, Mrs. Beck?"

Cousin Ted had bounced back and was protesting. "Now, look here, Charles, I am not an athlete. And I do not care to leave a loaded gun where this madman might get hold of it. I won't take that risk."

Tyler said, wearily, "Leave it empty."

Up on the balcony, Edie closed her eyes. A stupid man is a very dangerous man, she thought. How can Cousin Ted *be* so stupid? She began to feel helplessly angry.

The guard said, "Where now, Mr. Whitman?"

"Oh. Yes. Mrs. Beck, take this man with you, please. I want him to close and lock whatever can be closed and locked. And don't forget the cellar." Cousin Ted, inflated again, gave orders.

The tall housekeeper disappeared from Edie's view, and the guard followed her. Edie heard her say, "This is the cellar door." The only cellar to the house was beneath the turret. The door to the stairs, leading down, was well around the curve of the turret wall.

Edie was not only angry, she was beginning to realize what was happening here; she was frightened. But her anger spoke. She took three steps to the balcony rail and called down. "Cousin Ted, don't you know that he didn't 'escape'?"

"He's out! He's loose!"

"He was discharged."

"That's what I said. He's *out!* We know that."

Edie began to shake her head and she started down, to do battle with unreason. Granny's voice caught her and stopped her feet.

"Mercy! You're not thinking that he might have gotten *in,*" said Granny. "You mean while we were all away? Oh mercy!"

So the steam went out of Edie's anger.

"But I was here," she said, "and so was Mrs. Beck." Was she sounding nervous?

Granny was twisting around to peer at the housekeeper. "You didn't hear anything? In the shrubbery?"

Mrs. Beck said, "No, ma'am. Of course, I would only hear something at the back. Oh, I did hear the front doorbell. Miss Edith must have answered it."

Now was the time for Edie to say flatly, "Yes. It was Harold Page. I let him in. He's in my room." But she seemed to have lied, already. It was *not* the time for the truth. She set her legs to moving and sauntered down the remaining stairs. "Bell? Oh yes, just somebody . . . wanted something."

Cousin Ted turned with a shuffle of his small feet. "Get along," he snapped, over his shoulder. "Take him along, please."

So the housekeeper made a pointing gesture and the guard, who had evidently been down cellar, now closed the cellar door, turned the key in its lock, made an "after you" kind of gesture and followed her to the dining room.

Cousin Ted now came to Edie. He stood close and spoke low and his brown eyes behind his glasses were suspicious. "Edie, did you talk to the press?" he breathed at her.

"No, Cousin Ted, I did not," she said indignantly.

"For Wendy's sake, for all our sakes," he went on in the same ridiculously portentous manner, "we do not want scare headlines."

Edie shook her shoulders. "Mr. Tyler," she said boldly, "there *will* be headlines, if Cousin Ted shoots *anybody.*"

Tyler's voice had a weary authority. "She's right, Ted. Come on, now. Put the toy away."

"Actually, Ted," said Granny, "I don't believe you have fired a gun since you've had bifocals."

"Oh, Mother . . ."

Edie breathed in deeply. He was deflated. He took the very small handgun out of his jacket pocket and trotted reluctantly toward the big carved chest that stood under the balcony. He was going to put it away. Edie simply could not tell whether his mother had deliberately deflated him, as a means of control, or had done nothing at all but utter a stray

47

thought that had crossed her mind.

Edie's hope was not in them. She turned to Tyler. "Could I please speak to you, sir?"

"Go ahead." He did not budge.

"About Harold Page. Could I speak to you, alone?"

Charles Tyler took her in, with cold eyes. He knew who she was. A grand-niece. A social worker. He'd met social workers. He supposed they were earnest decent people; he didn't care for their bleeding hearts. This was a young one. He knew right away that she was going to defend the accused. And nuts to that.

"You know this man?" he said coldly. Her throat moved; her eyes winced. She didn't know the man. "You were here last night when this happened?" She'd been at some concert; she hadn't been here, last night, when it happened.

"Go ahead," he invited grimly. She didn't know anything.

Long ago, Charles Tyler had figured out a clear direction for himself. It was his business to apprehend a lawbreaker. What society then chose to do with same was not his business. Sometimes he felt like whoever it was that had to push some boulder up a hill forever. Or a housekeeper sweeping the dust with an old broom and watching the dust settle back again. They kept letting these kooks out. He'd pick them up and put them in and then they'd soon be out again. Look at this one, this kookie Harold Page. They'd had him in. By what kind of guess and gamble they'd let *him* loose, Charles Tyler did not know. Long ago, he had stopped trying to figure out the "whys" of this world. He was supposed to keep law and order. A man who got into a house that wasn't his, and beat up a woman, was a criminal. Whatever else he might be was not Charles Tyler's concern. He told himself all this quite often.

"I know," said the girl, "you want to pick him up." She smiled nervously.

Tyler didn't smile and didn't even answer. Good for her, he thought, if she knows that much.

"What will happen to him if you do?" she went on.

A blast of rage happened invisibly within Charles Tyler.

Ted Whitman, busily taking the ammunition out of his little gun, turned around to face them and puffed himself up. "Oh, he'll be put away, *at least*. Myra *Whitman* . . ."

That did it, for Tyler. How he wished to hell his sister had never mixed herself up with this bunch! She'd married the Whitman name, the house on the hill, the status and the money—and in the bargain had taken that spoiled kid, the stepdaughter, *and* her kookie ex. And now she was lying in the hospital. Why? *No* reason. And all her brother could do was sweep up this kook, not because his violence was senseless but because it was against the law. Put him in, again. And not because she was Myra *Whitman*.

"Myra *Tyler* Whitman," he said between his teeth. He gave Edie a glance like a knife to cut her head off. She'd be of the school that pleaded for the poor criminal who "hadn't known what he was doing." Charles Tyler didn't care whether he knew.

Charles Tyler cared whether he had done it.

"I don't think you need to worry, Edith," he said bitterly. "When I pick him up, he'll tell me everything he knows about what happened to my sister." If it takes a month, he was thinking. Oh, he'd sweep this one back into the dustbin. But *good*. He turned his back and gazed gloomily at the big tree.

Edie Thompson took a step backward. Dismayed. The Chief of Police had been coldly angry last night, but he had been giving orders, very busy, and the anger had seemed no more than natural, and well-controlled for what it was. It had blended with the confusion and everyone's consternation. But she *couldn't* talk to him, not now. She didn't dare. She thought he was in the clutches of a deep personal rage, an outrage. Whoever was suspected of having hurt his sister was going to be in for a very rough time. He had the power. And a suspect like Harold Page, so fitted to the crime, and so defenseless . . . No, she couldn't talk to the big policeman, now. And maybe never.

Not *she*. Edie knew that, somehow, the man was closed against her in particular. She sensed that. Couldn't think why. But it was paralyzing.

The big man turned again, his face fallen into an impassive gloom. "I'll get along now, Ted. I'll have a couple of men check the grounds, Mrs. Whitman."

He nodded, and started for the foyer.

Granny called after him, "Charles, you are very kind."

And Edie let him go. She went over to the table beyond the sofa where Mrs. Beck had put her tea. She sipped and found it hard to swallow. She didn't know what she was going to do.

She didn't follow Tyler out, to catch him in the driveway, to beg his objectivity as she confessed. She was afraid.

Wait. Think. Maybe . . . Edie now saw her project stretching out in time beyond her anticipation. Maybe—keep the boy hidden and safe while time worked and they *all* cooled off?

But how could she do that?

How could she do otherwise?

Chapter Four

The guard came back from the dining room-kitchen wing of the house, and Cousin Ted prepared to usher him to the east wing. This was the newer part of the house, in which Granny had her large and comfortable quarters and Ted and Myra the master bedroom, and Ted, his study.

Granny was stirring. "If he is going into my room," she announced, getting up in her spry way, "then so am I. I want him to look under the bed, quite thoroughly. I don't care for this idea that someone may be lurking. You have given me a very unpleasant picture, Ted, and I don't think it was very kind of you."

"Oh, Mother . . ."

Edie almost echoed him. It was a "Granny" speech, and unfathomable. She took a strong swallow of the cold tea. If they would only leave her alone in this room, *now*.

In fact, this room was often deserted. Perhaps because of the stairs, and the turret, this room was a kind of overgrown passageway. Nobody lived in it. Granny was in the habit of keeping to her own place where she had surrounded herself with an elegant clutter. Ted and Myra tended to use the solarium, incongruously so named, for it looked northerly, down the other side of the knoll and off to the sea. Wendy lived upstairs. That was her nest. It was usually some unhappy house guest, like Edie, who sat uncomfortably in this big cold place and wished she could find a book to read. There were no books in this room. There was no clutter, either. Sometimes there was a gathering here, before dinner, when there were dinner guests. The family did not gather here. In fact, the family did not gather.

So Edie had hopes that they would all vanish and she would have her chance. Maybe she could get the boy *out*—immediately.

But Cousin Ted was not vanishing, yet. He dawdled and turned back. He went trotting to the big carved chest and, while Edie watched him in dismay, he yanked open the top drawer and took out his beloved gun.

"Cousin Ted?" she croaked.

He turned and glared. He was going to reload. "If *I* see Harold Page, I do not intend to be helpless. I may not be as incompetent with a weapon as people think. Well?"

Well, she couldn't stop him. She said meekly, "I only wanted to ask you if you would please cash a check for me."

"Oh, Edie," on the puff of a sigh. "Not now."

"Then may I please borrow Myra's car?" (If Edie had a car, maybe she could get the boy into the car, somehow.)

"I am very sorry, Edie, but that car is quite new and Myra hates other people to drive it."

(Myra's in the hospital, thought Edie. She won't know. She *can't* care. I need a car.) "Then Wen-

53

dy's?" she said. "Do you know where her keys are?" (Wendy was off with Ronnie Mungo. Wendy didn't need a car.)

"No, I surely do not," said Cousin Ted, and then virtuously, "You must take that up with Wendy herself. Where do you want to go? I'm off to the hospital again in a few minutes. Drop you? If it's convenient."

He put the gun into his pocket. Edie said quietly, "Thank you, but it's not that important."

He started across the room to the east wing but something must have pinked him. He said to her, "How you can think of your own little concerns at all! Don't you realize what a terrible thing has occurred? Don't you understand that we are in great danger until this vicious madman is recaptured?"

Edie thought she could spit at him. "So is the whole population, too," she cried.

"What? What?"

"If *we* are," she raged, "if there is a vicious madman loose, then there *should* be scare headlines."

Cousin Ted raised his brows. "I will not be hounded by newspaper people. Really."

They stared at each other. It was Cousin Ted who said it. "Aren't you being rather stupid?" he said.

Somebody was shaking him by his shoulder, so he woke out of what was not quite sleep. It was that girl who wasn't Wendy. She was talking to him in a low angry voice; he could tell that she was not angry at him. She wanted him to sit up, put on his shoes, go somewhere with her. So he turned his legs, he pushed his torso, he sat on the edge of the bed with his feet to the floor, trying to banish those dizzying dreams or visions, those disconnected pictures, trying to see where he was and what was going on.

"It's the only chance," Edie was saying. "Right now. Quickly. Hurry. Before there is a guard out there. I'm going with you. I'll walk you out of here. If the police see the two of us walking together they won't think it's you. We can get out the front door right now. If you'll hurry . . ."

She went springing across the round room to her dresser; she seemed to be putting things into her purse. She had left his shoes on the floor, right under his eyes.

Harold looked down at four objects. Two shoes, two feet in gray socks. He closed his eyes and stretched up his brows and opened his eyes again. This was the turret room, that's right. The furniture looked as if it had been tossed in here, because it could not stand snug to the round. The strange tall narrow windows had blinds on them, against the glass, but there were no curtains. The glass was too far within the thickness of the wall. A crazy place.

He could hear her going on, in that low and furious voice, "No way to make them listen to anything. They are *impossible*. The only thing to do is get you away from here. Could you hurry?"

He looked down at his shoes and his feet. He reached for one of the shoes, but his hand fell. It wasn't necessary to try. He looked at the four objects. Two shoes, the same size. His left foot, looking a little larger. The right foot, outsized and impossible.

She said, close to his ear, "What's the matter?"

His hand swung, trying to point. "I can't . . ."

Her hand came down on his shoulder.

55

"I can't," he said. "My broken foot. I'll never . . ."

He felt her urgency die. Her hand began to press him back and he let it. He lay back. "I see," she said softly. "All right."

"I'm sorry. I just can't." He was very sorry that he couldn't do what she wanted him to do and put his shoes on.

She was like a nurse, now, or maybe his mother. She was helping him lift his legs back to the bed. She was pulling up the cover. She touched his forehead with a corner of the sheet, to wipe the perspiration away. "Never mind," she said. "How do you feel?"

"Oh, I'm better," he told her. "Much better. I feel a little woozy but I'm much, much better."

"Are you hungry? Are you thirsty?"

"I'm fine."

She sat down on the edge of the bed. This was a cool and quiet crazy place. They were lost in there—out of the world. But a sound came. The thin high ringing of a telephone bell, far far away.

"That's the telephone," she said quickly, as if she thought it might have frightened him. He lay looking at her profile, at the head held tensely on the twist of her neck. He could see the strain. He remembered her name, now. He was sorry to see her so strained and worried.

"You had better tell them where I am," he said calmly. "This isn't your trouble. You don't want to be in the middle, Edie."

Her head turned and she looked at him as if she marveled. Then, she smiled. "Oh, I'm not in the *middle*. I'm on your side."

56

He smiled up at her. He could see everything very clearly now, at least in his mind. "Just the same . . ."

"All right." She sighed. "But rest. Will you rest, a little while? Will you promise me? Don't make any noise? Don't stand too close to the windows? Then, I'll promise you that if I have to tell them, I'll give you warning first. Is that all right? A deal?"

"Deal. Only don't . . ."

"No, no, I won't," she said. "*I* won't be in too much trouble. I want to telephone somebody who'll come and help us both. Okay?"

"All right."

She touched him, giving him a comforting pat. She got up and went over to the dresser and took the band off her hair and began to brush it. Harold lay watching her with pleasure.

When Edie came out upon the balcony, Cousin Ted was there below with the guard, who was looking out the big window at the tree. "I see what you mean," he was saying. "That's quite a tree, ain't it? Pushing on the house, just about."

"It was planted by my grandfather," said Cousin Ted, importantly.

"A family tree? Right?" The guard, grinning at his own pleasantry, glanced up at Edie. "Don't worry about a thing, miss," he said cheerily. "Conrad's will take care of it."

Cousin Ted did not care for so much cheeriness. "Night and day, remember," he snapped. "I'm paying for it."

"Oh, sure thing, Mr. Whitman," Conrad said.

57

"I'm coming around to take night duty myself. I'll place the men now. Don't worry."

He knew he was dismissed and he saluted. Conrad had a little agency. He often supplied the guards at a wedding reception. He had done that for Mr. Whitman's wedding to his second wife. He was pleased with this job. He could charge a lot. (Night and day.) He was glad he was on the right side of Mr. Whitman. He went up to the foyer. He was gone.

Edie knew, as if he'd said so, that the guard was glad to be on the right side of Mr. Whitman.

Cousin Ted was patting his pockets, as if to check whether he had everything.

Edie ran down to him. "Cousin Ted, before you go, please—listen to me? It wasn't Harold Page who got in here."

"Oh ho," said Cousin Ted with an idiotic expression of joyous secrecy. "Indeed it was."

"Why?" cried Edie. "Because Wendy says she saw him? Cousin Ted, will you *think* about that, for just one minute? She saw him from her upstairs window—running, so she says. *Down* the drive. But she didn't do a thing about it. Wendy went to bed. *You* had to come home and find Myra . . ."

"She simply didn't realize at the time," said Cousin Ted. "Now—please tell Mrs. Beck—will you, Edie?—that I won't be home for dinner. I intend to stay with Myra as long as they will let me, which will be, I suppose, nine-ish. You'll be safe here without me, now."

"He was not here last night," said Edie loudly, spacing the words, insultingly.

"Who? What?"

"Harold Page. There's *no* reason to think so, except—"

"You don't know what you are talking about," said Cousin Ted with relish. "Charles Tyler just called me. They've found his bag. Oh, yes. Some small canvas affair. His name is on it. They found it in the shrubbery down at our gates. So you may as well stop talking nonsense, Edith. He was here, all right. But this is a fortress now. He can't get in again. Not alive."

His thin mouth was looking viciously satisfied. He left the house.

Up in the turret room, Harold got off the bed, took off his sweat-soaked, wrinkled white jacket. He hung it over the back of a chair. It might dry. He would have warning. He would rather not look too messy when he faced them. He limped toward the bathroom. Oh wow, his right foot was puffed up, pretty bad. Maybe he could soak it. Soma, he thought.

When he was in the cramped little bathroom, he was facing one of the windows, breast high, and he felt surprised to see the world out there, and the sun shining. It was kind of a shock to him. He blinked and stared and then his gaze came downward and he saw a man, standing a few yards from the corner of the house where the dining room was. He was just a man in a gray suit but—no, he wasn't, either. He kept moving, a little back and a little forth, and he kept looking around. He was a guard!

Harold's head cleared. It was as if the veils and

mists, through which all things had looked so dreamlike, melted away. Now he remembered, she had said there were guards, the girl had said so. Now that everything was clear and hard, Harold had the instinct to hide. He was in danger. There were guards down there and they were guarding. What? They were guarding the house against Harold Page. But Harold Page was *in* the house. It was kind of a joke on them, but it wasn't funny. Guns, she had said. He thought, I sure as hell better get out of here.

He went back to the round room and stole across to the opposite window, the one where the green leaves were pressing high on the window glass. He leaned cautiously into the embrasure. He couldn't see to his right, through so many leaves. He looked downward, to his left, and there was the big window and he could see into it and there was Wendy.

She was right down there, standing the way she always had stood, on her two feet at once and her feet apart. She was talking to somebody. There was another figure standing behind her. But Harold didn't look at it.

He looked a long time—about twenty seconds. He drew back and crossed the room and put himself down on the bed, on his back. He had expected to feel funny. He hadn't thought it would hit him quite so hard. He felt as if he'd been socked in the stomach. He had to understand this, now, and live through every bit of the pain. He had to let it hurt him. He'd learned this. He lay on his back with his wrist across his mouth.

Chapter Five

Schemes were racing through Edie's mind. She was standing beside the big carved chest, where the telephone was. Ought she to call the doctor at the Mental Hospital, this Dr. Wesley, the one who knew and had counseled Harold? He could help. He could say, for one thing, that Harold was not a madman, and for another, that he had not escaped. Surely he would be concerned, and would understand why Edie could not throw the boy to these wolves without trying everything else, first. He would understand what terrible damage might be done by a repetition of the same kind of injustice that had hurt the boy so much once before. He would be on Harold's side.

Or would it be best to call a lawyer, here? What lawyer? Or would it be best to call a cab, and just get Harold Page out of this house, maybe with the driver's help? Just face the guard down, and go. She could cash traveler's checks. Where could she go? With a boy who needed a doctor. To what doctor?

She was still standing beside the telephone when Wendy and Ronnie Mungo came in.

"What in the world is going on?" demanded Wendy, stopping by the window. "Daddy's got armed men around the house? How stupid!"

There she stood and Edie could feel herself pulling together with one clear purpose, to fight this enemy. She said, dryly, "Why? Aren't you afraid of the famous madman? Hi, Ronnie."

The man saluted. Wendy said, contemptuously, "Afraid of Harold? One word from me and he'd cry salt tears."

Wendy was nineteen now. She was pretty. Her hair was dark with certain reddish lights in it, and it was abundant, and it swirled prettily around her golden face, in which her eyes were the color of tea-in-a-cup without any cream. She was just a fraction of an inch shorter than Edie, but she wore very high heels on her very tiny feet. She wore bright colors. She wore, now, a yellow dress with green buttons down the front and a green scarf tucked in at the neckline. The dress was cotton and had cost as much as all of Edie's summer dresses put together. Wendy's figure was an hourglass. Edie's was the straighter, the daintier—yet Wendy made Edie feel faded and diminished. Poor.

Wendy was moody and the mood, for now, was pouting. She kept her back to Ronnie when she spoke. "Ronnie? Six-thirty?"

It crossed Edie's mind that Wendy's peers had never liked her, either, that she could remember.

"I take it we are going through with this dinner party?" said Ronnie Mungo in his pleasant tenor. He was as tall and elegantly made as ever, although not so young as when Edie (aged eighteen) had thought of him as an "older man." He had a well-practiced smile; he seemed as friendly as a puppy, in spite of his practiced manner of speaking, which took care to take nothing very seriously.

"It's supposed to be given *for* us," said Wendy sulkily.

"Well, fine."

Wendy threw her green purse on the sofa and herself after it. She was not pleased with life at the moment.

Ronnie came to lean on the back of a chair and take the cover off a candy box. His blue gaze slipped to Edie, who was standing her ground, who was not, this time, taking herself off with some small excuse to leave them together. He winked at her. "Our little flower," he said in a pseudo-confidence, "is drooping. . . ."

"Oh, shut up," said Wendy, who was drooping sulkily where she sat.

Edie looked away from the man's face, the one she had studied curiously, whenever the two of them had gone by, in these last few days. It was time to study Wendy.

Edie could feel herself hardening, feel herself gearing for battle. She knew exactly why she had, so soon and so easily, believed in Harold Page.

The time little Wendy, who had half a dozen cashmere sweaters, had taken Edie's one best one, and worn it, and torn it, and sworn she had never touched it. The time little Wendy had told her grandmother something. Edie was sure of it! . . . Because Wendy had wanted to go to Palm Springs for the weekend with her parents, but could not have gone unless they took Edie, too, to look after her. The very one-and-only weekend Edie had been supposed to have a date with Ronnie Mungo. And (get on, quickly) the time little Wendy had said she saw Edie in the solarium, on the morning that the parakeet had escaped from its cage and been destroyed by the cat. Time after time. Incident after incident.

Two kinds. The times when Wendy lied because she

63

wanted something, and the times when Wendy lied because she did not want to be punished for something she had done.

So Edie knew that Wendy was the enemy. Not Granny. Not Cousin Ted. Under the pressure of shock, after what had happened to Myra, they were merely being larger than themselves, Granny more maddeningly frivolous (or whatever you could call it) and Cousin Ted actively stupid instead of just bumbling about.

But it was Wendy who had put Harold Page into this affair, where he did not belong. He had nothing whatever to do with it, and Wendy knew that. Otherwise, why wasn't *she* afraid of him? There was a coincidence, of course. Harold had written to say that he was leaving the hospital on Monday. So Wendy had seized upon that, and the pattern that he fit so cozily, when she had lied last night.

Edie was hardening and at the same time flaming. Oh, Wendy was a liar, although she took care to lie only as often as it was wise to lie and continue to be believed. Edie did not doubt that she had lied to get her divorce and nearly wrecked the boy, that time. *This* time, she was not going to get away with it. By a saving coincidence, her cousin Edie happened to be here. Edie had not allowed the boy to walk into the trap and she would smash the lie and destroy the trap before she would give him up. But she had better not flame. Better be cool, be careful.

She said coolly, the latent anger almost hidden, "Myra is still in a coma, since you ask."

Wendy did not move an eyelash. Ronnie Mungo responded pleasantly. "She'll come out of it, won't she?"

Edie went nearer him. Let Wendy brood, *if* she was

64

brooding. "I guess so, Ron. Myra was in this room when you brought Wendy home last night? Did she say anything special?"

Ronnie tucked the candy into his cheek. "Myra? Well, we had a sparkling exchange, you know?" He sat on the arm of a chair and let his rump fall into the seat, so that his legs dangled. "Let me see. Myra said 'Good night.' And I replied. 'Good night,' I said." He grinned at her. Irreverence was his specialty. But Edie thought his bright eyes wondered what she could be wondering. Or did they guess?

"What did she say to you, Wendy?"

"Who? Nothing. I didn't listen." Wendy shifted and sat on her foot. "If Myra is going to be groggy all the rest of the summer," she said sullenly, "that's going to put the frost on a big wedding."

Ronnie said to Edie, as if this were an aside, one grownup to another, "This is the bother, you see?"

Is it? thought Edie. Is this *really* what's bothering her today? Are *her* moods swinging wider than ever? Is *she* larger than herself by the shock? More unreliable than her already unreliable self? She said aloud, "Myra can hardly help being what you call 'groggy.' "

"Oh, Cousin Edie," said Wendy, thrashing around, "that's not the point. I don't see why we need Myra at the wedding. She's not my real mother."

"She's a reasonable facsimile," said Edie, idly. She was thinking, No, Myra is not. Myra, to you, is nothing. Who is anything, to you? Are we going to find out?

Wendy said crossly, "Look, I'm trying to think."

You think, thought Edie. You just think, little cousin. Because somebody hurt Myra last night. The police found "signs of a struggle." And if it wasn't Harold Page, who was it then?

65

Ronnie Mungo listened to the silence shrewdly for a moment. Then he said, "I'm not so crazy about waiting at the altar in a white jacket while the bride comes down the aisle, like doom in lace. It's possible to have a 'little' wedding. Wait, I've got it. The word is 'quiet'?"

Wendy swiveled her dark head and sent him a long stare.

"Or," he said, shifting his long legs to lie stretched out in the chair, "maybe you want to call the whole thing off? Another day, another bridegroom? In which case, we better not make an announcement at this party. Or even go."

He sounded as if he didn't care. Maybe, to get along with Wendy, you had to seem to care even less than she. Edie sat down, to listen.

"I wanted the whole show." Wendy pouted. "The cake and the flowers. And eight bridesmaids."

"And the veil?" said Edie, her anger slipping. "Which, I presume, you missed, the first time around."

"Edie, will you kindly . . ." Wendy sounded exasperated, but only as if with a fly. "*She* never got married at all, Ron. And what are you, Edie . . . twenty-five?"

"Withering on the vine," drawled Edie. She settled into the chair.

Wendy got up and crossed to the solarium doors and stood there with her back to them.

Ron said in a moment, casually, "So you're a social worker now? Get a bang out of that, do you, Cousin Edie?"

"In a way," said Edie slowly. She was trying to cool down.

"Doing good, eh? I don't understand that sort of

thing, believe me." He was playing with his key case, tossing and catching it.

Edie said sweetly, "I believe you." He was an attractive man, to women. He must be, thought Edie. He's been married twice already. Why did his wives divorce him? Something dark moved in her blood as she wondered.

But Wendy turned around and came waspishly back into the conversation. "Why are you trying to understand *her?* It's me you're going to marry."

"Oh? Then it's on?" said Ron, lightly.

Wendy was full of storm. "If we're not going to have a big wedding, what is there to wait for?"

"Okay," he said. "How about tomorrow?"

Edie could see Wendy's face changing and she gasped, "Wendy, you can't."

"I most certainly can," said Wendy coldly. "The divorce is final. I'm of age, now. I will get my mother's trust money when I marry. And I have spelled it out and spelled it out and I'm not going to spell it out anymore. Because I *can* . . . if I want to."

She went prancing across the carpet on her tiny feet, like a child in a tantrum.

Edie said, frowning, puzzled, "With Myra in the hospital—"

"So much the better," snapped Wendy. *"She* doesn't particularly want me to marry Ronnie."

Does she not? thought Edie. Does she not, indeed? And when was it that you spelled it out so many times?

Ron got up and moved toward Wendy. His pleasant voice, with its constant undernote of mockery, might have been designed to tease. "Ah now, naturally, I am not good enough *for* you. But the old folks *will* be reconciled, in the end." He was reaching for her. But

Wendy stepped away.

"Tomorrow?" she said coldly.

"Well, no," he answered, quickly serious. "As a matter of fact, we can't get the red tape cut that soon."

"But we can get our blood tests tomorrow."

"True."

"Can we get on a plane to Paris? I mean *soon*. After the whatever-it-is . . . the three days?"

"Should be possible. I'll see."

"All right, Ronnie."

Edie sat marveling at this exchange, so cold, so coldly decisive. She began to think that Granny was right. These two would suit each other very well.

Now Wendy was softened and she kissed the man's cheek lightly. "Go away, now. Be back by six-thirty and we'll go to this party."

"Have to take one of those bodyguards along?" he said, with a mock shudder.

"Of course not," said Wendy. "How would Harold know where I was? Anyway, maybe they've caught him by now and put him back where he belongs."

"I won't worry about it if you don't, sunshine," Ronnie said. "So long, Cousin Edie. Do good, now."

Edie said thoughtfully, "I'll try."

When he had gone, Wendy seemed to think herself alone. She didn't look at Edie. She went prancing toward the door to the long dining room and sent her high voice calling, "Becky? Beck-*yyy?* Come here, will you?" She didn't wait for an answer, but turned.

Edie said, with the deadliest calm she could manage, "Wendy, when you marry Ronnie Mungo, what are you going to do with the baby?"

68

"The what?" said Wendy.

"Your child. Your son."

There may have been a flush under the golden skin of the pretty face. But Wendy said flatly, "He is deaf as a stone. How could I do anything with him? Somebody will have to take care."

"What does Ronnie say, about the baby?"

Wendy was staring at her. "Not a word. We don't discuss it." Then she whirled to turn her back. "Didn't she *hear* me!"

"What," said Edie, in the same deadly tone, "is your idea of marriage, I wonder?"

Now Wendy turned again and she was smiling lopsidedly, lips closed, one end of the mouth tucked up into the flesh of the cheek. "It depends on the one you marry."

"I remember Ronnie from a long time ago," said Edie, feeling blind.

"I'll *bet* you do," her cousin said.

"He was a pretty spectacular playboy, way back then. When I was eighteen, I cried all night. Maybe you remember? *Somebody* had told your grandmother *something*."

"Way-back-then?" said Wendy, insultingly. She wasn't going to admit anything.

"How old is he now? And how many wives?"

"He's thirty-four," said Wendy. Her temper flared. "And who cares how many wives. He hasn't got one *now*. What in the world is your idea of marriage? You should try it sometime." She seemed to dance impatiently. "Oh, where is that old idiot? I want her to press my yellow dress. Money is the thing, you know, Edie. Too bad you'll have to wait for yours, until Granny dies."

Edie was lost. "Ronnie Mungo has money, you

mean?"

"I'll have money, is what I mean," said Wendy. "Of my own."

Edie was stumped, really stumped. Money would have been the last thing to cross Edie's mind. Mrs. Beck came bustling and Wendy said, "Oh, there you are, Becky. You come on up."

Mrs. Beck's long-jawed face was looking perfectly foolish with devotion. "Yes, lamb. Yes, love."

"I'm going to the party," said Wendy, on the stairs.

"It will do you good. Do you good, lamb," said Mrs. Beck, drawn upward behind her.

Edie sat still, where she was. She had not missed, of course, the obvious fact that Mrs. Beck was Wendy's slave. She remembered mentioning something like that, and how Granny had said, in Granny's way, "Oh, Mrs. Beck's been raising Wendy. After all, if *she* was willing, why should *I?*"

But this was not to the point, really. The point was, how could Edie protect a country boy—rather a pathetically unlucky boy, a boy who was not in the best physical condition to defend himself—from these terrible people? In particular, from Wendy Whitman, who had lied, would lie, being possessed, as far as Edie could tell, of no scruples at all. Which of the household could she approach, to ask for mercy and understanding, or even a mind open to the reestablishment of justice? And, if none, what could she do for Harold Page?

Mrs. Beck came swiftly down, a yellow dinner dress over her arm. Wendy's in a yellow mood today, she was thinking. Ah, yellow suits her. She reached the bottom of the stairs and was starting for the

70

kitchen regions, when Miss Edith called her name.

"Yes, Miss Edith?" Mrs. Beck had very little time for Edie.

"Mr. Whitman asked me to tell you that he won't be here for dinner."

Good, thought Mrs. Beck. "I see," she said aloud, "Thank you. Miss Wendy won't be here either." She was counting in her mind; that left the old lady and this Edith. This Edith spoke again.

"Mrs. Beck, you were in the house last night when it happened? You didn't hear anything at all?"

"My room is at the back," said Mrs. Beck. "I don't hear." (Let her believe that.)

"What about the doorbell?" Edie said, quick to remember.

"I don't," said Mrs. Beck, frowning judiciously, "recollect hearing the doorbell. Of course, I woke up, later on . . ." Now, it occurred to her that she might find out something. She tossed the dress over one shoulder and began to move around the room, straightening this and that. "I am behind in the work," she sighed, "with the maids away." Selma was having a bout with the flu and Angie was on vacation. Mrs. Beck was not sorry that they happened to be away.

"Miss Myra *is* going to be all right?" she said. "Don't they say?"

"They say so." Edie was standing. With pants on, at this hour! Mrs. Beck could not approve. Then Edie said, "Do you believe it was Harold Page?"

"Why, Miss Wendy saw him." Mrs. Beck swooped upon a bit of white, tucked between the cushions and the arm of a big chair. It was a paper napkin. She began to pleat it in her hands.

"So she says." Edie was speaking with a nervous air

71

of Suspicion. "Of course, Miss Myra will be able to tell us the truth very soon. It may have been some other—madman."

Mrs. Beck knew that her eyes were turning. She let out a sigh. "I'm very upset about Miss Myra. To think . . . in the hospital!" She clicked her tongue. "I wish I could go see her for myself."

"Why not?" said Edie.

"There's only two for dinner. I wonder if I could take the evening . . ."

"Mr. Whitman's going to be at the hospital until the evening visiting hours are over."

(Ah!) Mrs. Beck said, "Oh, I see." She started toward the kitchen again. Had to press the dress. And think about this.

But Edie had something else on her mind. "Mrs. Beck, were you here when there was that other trouble? When Harold Page was supposed to have beaten Wendy?"

(Supposed to have?) Mrs. Beck felt like letting out a piece of her mind. "Oh, she had to be rid of *him,* Miss Edith. Had to be rid of *him.* He was not for her. She ran away, for the fun of it, you know. So young. But I couldn't approve."

Maybe she shouldn't have said that. It wasn't supposed to be for her to approve. Mrs. Beck's kingdom was in secret.

"You do approve of Ronnie Mungo?" the girl was saying.

"That's different." Mrs. Beck was glad to be telling the truth. "Mr. Mungo is a man-of-the-world. And I'll be with her, you know. He's promised me. Why, we'll travel. Do her good to get away from here." Yes, away from the old lady, and the silly man, the clever stepmother, the gloomy old house. And the town,

72

too.

"Why," Edie was asking, "didn't Wendy 'get away' to college? Or take a job?"

A *job!* Mrs. Beck felt shocked. But how ridiculous! "What would *she* take a job for, Miss Edith? That's not for *her.* She needs to be gay and enjoy herself, the pretty thing. Oh, I understand her. Poor little mother-less child." (My child.) "Oh, she has suffered."

"She has?" Miss Edith was not believing. "How do you feel," the girl said angrily, "about the poor little motherless, fatherless baby?"

Mrs. Beck knew how she felt and she said it. "Oh, now that was *very* hard on Wendy. To bear a child that wasn't *right.* Oh, poor lamb! So hard! But we've put that behind."

She began to stroke the fabric of the dress. She was talking too much. Well, she had a lot on her mind. She said, "Pretty, isn't it? Does need pressing. I must hurry." So much to do. So much to think about.

Edie said, loudly, "*I* don't believe Harold Page was here last night at all."

Mrs. Beck stopped in her tracks. She turned and made her mouth humble and her voice gentle to correct. "Why, he must have done it, Miss Edith. Poor crazy person. I'm sure he didn't know what he was doing." She thought of another point to make. "Miss Myra might have brought it on herself, you know. Not knowing how to handle him." Mrs. Beck would have known how to handle him.

"We'll find out," Edie said, "when Miss Myra wakes up."

Mrs. Beck was glad to hear Wendy screaming down the stairs. "Becky! I can't find my gold slippers."

Her gold slippers? Oh, yes, on the shelf. Mrs. Beck could put her hand on them. "I'll find them, lamb,"

73

she called upward. "As soon as I can, love. Don't you worry."

She said to Miss Edith, sternly, "Excuse me."

Now then, through the long dining room, into the big square kitchen, pull down the ironing board. So much to do. Sometimes Mrs. Beck thought that she, and she alone, had to handle the whole world and all the people in it.

Edie sat down in a chair feeling frightened and small. Wendy would lie; Mrs. Beck would back her up, whatever Wendy chose to say. The woman had made Edie's skin crawl. No hope there. Still, nothing was any worse, or any better either, since Wendy had gone upstairs. Not really. Was it? Why did Edie have the feeling that she herself had just done something she ought not to have done, something dangerous? Why was she feeling frightened?

Chapter Six

At a quarter of midnight, the prisoner came out of the turret room with his hair combed neatly, and his white coat on. He came down the stairs on his stockinged feet and told Edie that he was going to give himself up, now.

She sat up on the sofa and began to try to talk him out of it.

The big room was dim; there was only one lamp burning. The house was very quiet. It was safe enough to talk here, safer than the turret room, perhaps, the guard being where he was. Granny slept without her hearing aid. Cousin Ted had retired long ago and was asleep in his bedroom, beyond the study, far at the end of the east wing. Mrs. Beck's room was away at the back. She might not have come in yet, but even if she had, she would not hear soft voices.

No one could see in. The doors to the solarium were closed. A night light burned in the foyer; Wendy was still out. But the only window in the foyer was well around the wall. Velvet draperies were drawn across the big window and they were heavy. They did not cover the highest part where the glass went up into an arch, but the tree obscured that section. Black leaves made a pattern against the silver night. No one's angle of sight could come through there and strike down to where they were.

Edie was sitting up on the sofa wearing a short nightgown with its matching peignoir. She had her slippers on her feet although they were covered by the big, soft, puffy, flowered quilt. She had thought she would sleep down here. (If there was such a thing as sleep.) If anyone ordered her to her room, she would simply go. So it was safe enough. It had seemed safer to be more or less on guard, outside that door.

She had stolen some food for Harold Page at dinnertime. After he had eaten, he had fallen asleep. Edie had held some hope for darkness, but the moon was up, too soon, too bright.

There was little hope, anyhow. Edie had spotted the positions of the guards and they had been well placed. The man on the dining room corner could see, along two sides of the house, both the kitchen door and the outside cellar door, at the base of the turret. The guard on the corner of Cousin Ted's study could see the whole back terrace; there was no way to slip out of the solarium and across that bare expanse to the shrubbery, unseen. The guard near the big tree could see the front door and the driveway turnaround. That took care of doors. As for windows, there was no sliding down the turret wall, no getting out by using the tree, and on the other windows, no shutter could wag and wag unseen. To be caught *getting out of a window* would be madness. These men had guns.

Someone far more intelligent than Cousin Ted had placed those guards to keep Harold Page out of this house. They were equally well placed to keep him in.

She had not attempted to walk him out boldly, by daylight. She was sure that the guard would query a shoeless man, and the boy's weakness and illness would be too obvious. No such exit could seem casual. So she did not dream of trying to walk him out by this moonlight, either. He must stay until morning. It was safer and there were other ways to help him.

But her prisoner was restless.

She said to him now, "Dr. Wesley will call me back in the morning. They promised me. I left *my* name. And please let me try again with Mr. Tyler? In the morning? It would be better if I could get to him. He's the Chief of Police, and even if he felt like torturing a confession out of you, he wouldn't do that. I mean, it isn't done. He scared me this afternoon. I shouldn't have let him scare me. I do think I might get him to listen. Are you cold?"

The boy leaned on the back of the sofa and was shuddering.

"*I'm* scared," he said gravely, "but the one who scares me . . ."

She read his mind. "Wendy's at a party," she said, a little bitterly. "She'll be a while, but please go back. Please wait?"

His head shook a slow negative.

She said, "I wish you hadn't left your bag outside, you know. *That's* made things worse." She was feeling a little annoyed, because she wanted to save him so much more than he seemed to want to be saved.

"I want to get it over with, *before* Wendy comes," he said. "I feel, you know . . . somehow or other . . . I'll never, never . . . She can always beat me."

No, she can't, thought Edie. Not this time.

"Oh, come on. Cheer up," she pleaded. "Please.

77

We've gone this far." He wasn't agreeing. He was leaning on his elbows, with his hands clasped lightly. He had good hands. His young face was grave. "Were you in love with her, Harold?" Edie asked.

"Oh, yes."

"Wendy can be very attractive."

"I know," he said. He smiled at her. He wasn't jittery. He didn't seem to be afraid. He was chilled, and feverish. "I came up here on leave with a few of the fellows that time," he began. "We hung around the beach. And here came Wendy Whitman and she chose me. Well, I suppose I believed in chemistry or love at first sight or something corny." He didn't sound bitter about it. He was just remembering. "I really did believe that it was so. Just two days, and then we were tearing down to the border in Wendy's car and she drives like a racer. Oh Lord-ee, it was wonderful! We got into Mexico. We lied about our ages. We got married. We found this motel. I thought to myself, Boy, now you have got everything in the whole world. You have got it all."

His hands were quiet. Edie thought, Oh the poor kid, why did he have to meet Wendy Whitman? *Ever?*

"But my leave wasn't lasting forever," he said, shifting to lean sideways, "so we came back here."

"Was the family upset?" Edie tried to imagine. *This* boy openly in this house.

"They didn't seem to be, not too much," he told her. "They seemed a little bit stiff toward me but I thought that was only natural. Nobody chewed me out."

"Cousin Ted and Myra weren't married yet, were they?"

"No, but they were engaged. Myra was here all the time. They were fussing about *their* wedding. Listen,

78

I was so doggoned silly happy, I didn't really notice anything. I had to go back to camp the next day, and I went. On a big fat pink cloud. Next leave I could get, it was the same. I didn't see them much. Talk to them much. Notice much. Wendy was going to come and live near the Post. We were making plans"—his eyes flicked to her face—"that is, when we bothered. But she put that off and put it off and those plans . . . just died. It seemed to get to be too late. Actually, after Wendy got pregnant . . ."

Now his eyes were blind. "Yes?" she prodded.

"She was moody," he said, quietly. "Mustn't touch. Then I saw I was . . . I was like a piece of furniture that somebody had left around the house. They'd act as if 'Oh, yes, that's Harold, isn't it?' And they'd walk around me. As if they didn't see me or hear me unless I got in the way. And it kept getting worse."

His face seemed to be drawn fine with the memory of that incomprehensible misery. But he drew himself up a little. "You see, Wendy didn't like being pregnant. She hated that. She gloomed around. Or she'd snap at me or get in a temper over nothing. Well, I tried to be patient and all that stuff. It was a mystery to me."

Edie's heart hurt. Oh you poor kid, she was thinking, you've been taken. You've been cheated. You're too innocent.

"When the baby was born," he was going on, "they didn't even—*I* called *them* and then they told me. So I came, as soon as I could get a pass. That's when they let me hold him, that once." He brooded a moment. "And when I finally left this town, when it was all over but the proceedings, I went, sitting in the back of some truck, and I was crying and swearing. I thought I'd *never* be back. Well. But I have a son, and

79

whatever *they* think, I hold myself responsible."

Edie was pierced; this seemed to her so comical and so sad.

She thought, Somebody has to tell him. She said as gently as she could, "Harold, I don't know whether you've ever thought of this . . ."

But he straightened, and he grinned down at her.

"Sure I've thought of it, and so has everybody else. It's the first thing *to* think of. Sounds just as if she needed a husband in a hurry? But he's *my* baby, all right."

Oh no, you are wrong, she was thinking. They fooled you and it was wicked.

"If that was the truth of it," the boy went on, "I could have figured it, you know. Not that I wouldn't have been plenty burned, but I'd see they had some kind of a reason."

"Are you sure of the birth date?" Edie pressed. "You say they didn't call you."

"That was because I didn't matter." He looked down at her somberly. "The ears? Hereditary in my family? I guess you forgot."

"I guess I did," she murmured. Her face felt hot. He wasn't as innocent as she had assumed and nobody was. She had been innocent to assume . . .

"So how is it to be understood?" he asked her, and she had a funny feeling that, in this moment, he was older than she. "Do you know?"

"There's probably nothing to understand," said Edie hotly, "except that Wendy is spoiled rotten and always has been. Or"—she began to struggle with her own ideas—"not so much spoiled as . . . I don't know. But they shut themselves up here. In a tower. They have their own version of the world and other people. Other people don't count much. They don't

80

even care about each other, *very* much, but they still are the only ones who count at all. And you can't change them. It used to infuriate me. Genevieve, Wendy's mother, was alive then, and she was a silly woman. You know, I work with real people, who pay attention, at least sometimes. But the Whitmans . . . Well, I know exactly what you mean about being made to feel as if you were some old box in this house, to be stumbled over.

"Wendy . . ." She paused to say this carefully. "I'll tell you one thing. Their idea of Wendy is set, like concrete. No matter what she does, she is their pretty, sensitive little Wendy, then, and now, and forever more. Their idea of me is set, too. I am unfortunate and have to be fed. It got so . . . I had to get away. I couldn't grow. I was going to lose my sense of being anything."

He was listening gravely. He seemed to be understanding what she could not quite express. This is a nice boy, thought Edie, and her anger rose.

"The truth is," she cried, "Wendy always did get away with murder!"

"*Ssh.*" His eyes had winced.

"Did you hear something?" she whispered.

"I don't know. I guess not." He had lowered his head. "Look, Edie, I'm going out there now and surrender to the guard in front. It's the best thing and the best time."

"Don't. Don't," she cried. "*I'm* scared."

He seemed sorry to hear this. "Ah, no. Why?"

"How do I know he won't shoot you down?" she chattered. She did not want him to give up. She did not want him to be beaten. By Wendy.

"Would you like to go first, then?" he suggested. "I guess he wouldn't shoot *you* down . . . not in that

81

outfit." He was smiling.

"I don't want you to do it at all," she insisted. "Not yet. Maybe there'll be a better way. If your Dr. Wesley would only come. He'd stand up to them. At least, he wouldn't let them hurt you."

"It wouldn't matter if they hurt me," Harold said.

"Yes, it would." She saw that he swayed. "Do you feel dizzy still?" She reached up to touch his forehead. It felt dry and hot, but not as hot as it had been. He was shivering.

"I guess you don't see why," he said.

"Come. Sit," she pleaded. "You shouldn't be chilled. Tell me." She thought, I am doing wrong not to get him to a doctor. But oh, not a prison doctor.

He moved around the sofa, limping, and sat down beside her. As she held up the quilt to let him sit, and tucked it back over his lower body, she thought, I could hide him, right where he is, if anybody comes. I don't want him to go out there and have the guards whistling and shouting and calling the police. I don't want him pushed around. Or headlines in the papers, "berserk ex-husband." He's had enough.

"It's bad," he said seriously. "Listen, I said I was scared of Wendy. But that's not quite it. Oh listen, Edie"—she felt him trembling—"I loved her. I was crazy about her. And she hurt me worse than anybody ever . . . The thing is, now I'd like to hurt her. Oh, I sure would. So, see, she's still there between me and . . . and being all straightened around. I hate her and I love her, so much . . . I don't think I'd dare to meet her, even. I would like to beat her, Edie, until she notices that I'm alive. And that's the truth that I'm afraid of."

"I know it's hard. I know," cried Edie instantly. "But don't let her—"

82

"Look, I'm not a vegetable," he burst, "and she's telling a lie again, and it makes me plenty mad. But I don't *want* to hit her, either. So you see, I'd better go."

To Edie, in the moment, the whole situation became even more explosively dangerous than she had, until now, believed it to be. She knew she ought never to have hidden Harold Page in the turret room. She ought to have made him go away, the moment she had realized who he was. Perhaps she ought never to have interfered at all, but called the police herself. Been the good citizen. Washed her hands. No one would have blamed her. She seemed, instead, to have made herself judge and jury, although she was prejudiced, and had insufficient evidence, and took risks. The fact that the boy was aware of his present impulse toward violence did not deny that it was there.

Edie didn't yet believe that he had beaten anyone, nor did she quite believe that he ever would. But there had been violence in this house, and now she could feel the threat of future violence to be hanging most dangerously over it. Everyone seemed to have been swinging far out, along an exaggeration of his own tendencies. Something was going to crash; something would be smashed and hurt.

"You don't have to meet Wendy," she said to him. "I won't let you meet her. I only want to get you completely out of all this miserable . . ."

The still air seemed to eddy. *"Don't* come in, if you don't want to." Wendy's living voice rang with hostility.

The boy turned his whole body; a look of terror was on his face. His hand clawed at the back of the sofa and slipped. With a complete swinging out of her own emotions, at the first sound of Wendy's voice, Edie pushed at him. He slid to his knees on the floor. His head burrowed into the sofa seat, as she pushed it down. She had time to whisper ruthlessly, "Don't let *me* be caught like this." This was her wits in service to the surging of her will. Use anything, use his pity, to made him hide, so that Edie Thompson could snatch, from Wendy Whitman, her prey.

She took the edge of the quilt in her right hand and swung her arm. The lightweight quilt billowed and settled. He was hidden. She could feel the weight of his arm over her folded knees. She folded her own body, in order to scrunch down and rest her head below the top of the sofa-back.

She heard Ronnie Mungo's mocking voice. "Don't know when I've heard a more gracious invitation."

She heard the front door thud shut. She heard Wendy's golden heels, tapping on the tile. She heard her own blood in her ears.

It was warm and safe, where Harold was hidden. He had a wonderful sense of comfort and safety. He knew that he was in a place where he did not have to do anything at all. He also knew where he was, the way Dr. Wesley would say it.

"Why can't we?" Wendy's mood was stubborn. "That's what you haven't explained."

Edie kept her head low. She couldn't see them. But they were in the room.

Ron said, "It may be a hell of a long drive, but not that long. If we start out now, we arrive too damn early in the morning." His patience was on the edge of indifference. "And excuse me, my sunshine, but getting married in the first faint dawn—"

"Oh, stop clowning," Wendy snapped.

"Why rush into this, then?" His voice became mild and colorless. "It wouldn't 'look well,' would it?"

"Another day, another bride?" Wendy was sharp.

"I didn't say that. If you want a rough translation, why offend your wealthy grandmother? She isn't willing *all* the money to your cousin, is she?"

Neither of them spoke, for a moment, and Edie was forced to breathe. Then Wendy said, "But Ronnie . . ." in such a tone as to make Edie swallow hard. If there was going to be any canoodling, all of Edie's essentially puritanical soul writhed at the thought of eavesdropping.

"Hey," she croaked, "I'm sorry, but I'm here."

She heard a harsh rustling and then Wendy's furious face was looking down at her. "What are you doing there?"

"I was trying to sleep. Excuse it, please." Edie tried to be flip.

Ron spoke, behind her. "What *have* we here, an honest woman? Didn't care to listen in on two such turtle doves?" Was he laughing? Edie rolled her eyes up and saw his face, upside down. "What's the matter, Edie, honey? Scared of the bogeyman?"

"Well, you can just get yourself up and trot yourself to your bed." Wendy was giving orders.

"No," said Edie, faintly.

"NO!" It was a shriek.

So Edie unfolded her body enough to sit higher, keeping a tight clutch on the quilt. She felt very steady and not much afraid. You never heard that word before, she thought, did you, little cousin? To herself she said, with resolution and despair, No, I will not expose him and humiliate him and give him up, until I absolutely have to. I will probably have to. But not this minute. Or the next.

The telephone rang.

Edie said, clearly and sharply, "But if I get up and go to my room, then I'll crack my door and listen to everything you say or do and take down notes." It was childish, but Wendy was childish. Edie was ready to fight with Wendy, childishly, physically, any way that seemed necessary. She thought, Even if I lose, Ron wouldn't hurt him. She thought, This can't last many more seconds, but I'll make it last as long as I can. She found herself nourishing a little hope that Ronnie Mungo would see, would help, if Wendy went into a real tantrum.

The phone rang again. "She's got a nice little black-mailing technique there," drawled Ron, sounding amused. "*I'm* taking notes, sunshine. Go on, answer the phone."

As the phone rang for the third time, the ring choked off.

Edie was blinking with surprise. She wiggled her stiff body even higher and twisted to see where they were. Wendy had gone to the phone and stood with the instrument in her hand, although evidently too angry to speak into it. Ron was sauntering toward a chair, and as Edie twisted far enough around to see him plain, he grinned at her and perched on the chair arm. Does he know? she thought. And if so, is he helping me?

"By the way," he said, as benign as an old gentleman of Victoria's day, "you look very pretty."

Edie felt terrified. "I'm sorry," she murmured.

"Not I." His smile crinkled.

Did he think he was pleasing her? Her hands still tight on the quilt, Edie bowed her head. "Don't tease me," she begged, and thought to herself, But he is teasing Wendy, of course.

Oh, Lord, get us out of this? Her knees had shifted. She wondered briefly whether the boy was there. He was completely hidden. It was as if he existed only in her imagination.

Wendy said into the phone, "Yes? . . . Oh yes, Doctor."

Doctor! Well, there it goes, thought Edie. It must be Dr. Wesley, calling back, too soon. She would have to move; she would have to speak to him. She had a prevision of the quilt, rising uncannily, and then falling away from the boy, and people screaming.

Wendy said, "Oh yes, this is her stepdaughter . . . No, I think he's . . ." She took the instrument from her ear and said to Edie, "Where is Daddy?"

Edie said, "Asleep, I imagine. He said he'd take his phone off."

Question and answer were commonplace. They were spoken in an intermission, commonplace, outside of fear, outside of rage, outside of stratagem, outside of war.

Wendy purred into the phone. "He is asleep. Must I disturb him? . . . Oh, I see . . . Yes, I will . . . Thank you, Doctor."

She hung up and hugged her short white wrap. Her yellow skirt fluttered. Edie had a sudden hope.

"Anything . . . ?" she cried.

"Myra's scheduled for surgery at *six* A.M. instead of seven. He just wanted to let us know." Wendy was sullen.

Ron said, "Want me to wake your father?"

"Oh, why?" said Wendy. "No use to go down there now."

"Was she conscious?" said Edie. "Did she speak?"

This was her hope. Maybe the whole thing was over!

"How can she speak," said Wendy, furiously, "until they fix whatever's the matter with her? Edie, if you don't begin to mind your own business, and not everybody else's, I'll tell Daddy to throw you out. And he will, too."

"I don't doubt it," murmured Edie, scrunching down.

"Go to *bed*."

"Don't you tell me what to do, Wendy, please." Another prevision: Wendy peeling the quilt away and the boy, exposed, cowering. Helpless. Crying salt tears. No.

But Ron, who was back of her head and unseen now, said, "Why don't *you* go to bed, Wendy, and sleep that off?" His voice was flat.

"Sleep what off?"

"Whatever foul mood you're in. I'm not driving to Mexico with *it,* I'll tell you. Matter of fact, *I'm* going to bed."

Edie could see the tea-colored eyes narrowing. "Alone?" said Wendy, nastily.

Ron said, "It could be." Unperturbed.

He must be going. Wendy was being drawn away. Edie found that her head could turn. They were close to the steps to the foyer. Her hands relaxed on the quilt, and dared to lift it, just a little. If he was there, could he breathe? He was there. Her fingers touched his cheek. He was breathing, quietly. She could feel his breath on her hand. She pressed two fingers into his cheek, and tried to send a silent message. Be still. Wait.

And strained to hear what they were saying.

"Well? Are we getting our blood tests tomorrow, or are we not?" Stormy.

"Just in case, eh?" Ron's voice was its normal faintly mocking drawl. "Why not, then?"

"So, in three days? Or never?" Wendy seemed to be threatening. There was a brief silence.

Then Rod said, "Or sooner? You can drive to Mexico by daylight, you know. In a sunnier frame of mind. Tomorrow?"

"If you are here early. And I mean early." Still threatening.

"And if not?"

Edie could hear no answer.

"Then never, eh?" he said, with light acceptance. "Right. I'll sleep on it." His voice became louder. "Good night, Cousin Edie. I'm sorry if I teased you."

"Sleep well," said Wendy grimly.

He was gone and Edie was trembling. Who would help her, now, to cope with Wendy? The guard, she thought. I can always call for him. But maybe . . . Maybe. "Good night, Wendy," she said on a yawn, with good hope.

Let Wendy go up to her own nest. Let the boy go back to his safe prison. Let everything hold, simply hold, the way things were.

Chapter Seven

Ronnie Mungo's headlights illuminated the figure of Mrs. Beck, just as she was turning into the path that led around the house. She knew who it was; Wendy was in, then. She tried to walk a little faster.

The moon was up. The flagstone path was clear. The night air was pleasantly cool and her dark coat was comfortable. She said, "Good evening," to the first guard. To the second guard, at the dining room corner where she must turn, she said something about a double feature being much too long. She noted, with satisfaction, the relaxed friendliness of their responses. Evidently, there had been no excitement here. They had seen no madman.

She took from her handbag the back door key and the paper napkin which she meant to destroy. She had chosen to bring it with her, all the way home, because across the corner was printed the Whitman name. She had every right to have it. And all was well, now.

Charles Tyler said to his wife, "Could be, he suicided. That's where the 'berserk' ones are usually headed." Heading for oblivion, he was thinking. *They* don't believe in heaven or in hell. What do they care how many innocent souls get hurt on their way? People who jump off buildings, and never mind what decent citizen is minding his business on the street below. Or what cop has to risk his life, either. People who turn on the gas and blow out the wall, and never mind who might be living his inoffensive life on the other side of the wall. Kooks. Augh . . ." He stretched in anger.

There used to be the good old days in crime, he mused. Criminals who went professionally about *their* business, with understandable motives. They wanted money that they hadn't earned in the common market. So, they'd have a project. Took intelligence, of a kind. But not so much anymore. Now it was the kooks, infesting the world. And breeding like maggots. Violence for violence's sake. For no gain, *all* loss. Sometimes he sure felt he'd like to give *them* violence, but he knew that was old-fashioned and useless. He could be as sorry for some poor kook as anybody else—but if one of them broke the law, then he broke the law. If that wasn't clear, then Charles Tyler didn't know where he was.

"Guess I'm getting old," he mumbled.

His wife patted him. She herself had never liked his sister Myra, a cold and greedy little package if Josie Tyler had ever seen one. It didn't matter what Josie felt, but she suspected it mattered that Charles had never much liked his sister, either. He'd be feeling guilty for it now.

Josie said, "You'll get him."

"Whatever that'll mean," he grumbled.

"That means you'll get him, because you are good, and you will," said Josie loyally, and thought, Poor Charles. Poor Charles. "Go to sleep," she soothed.

Two police cars kept circling the neighborhood of the Whitman house, using spotlights on the shrubbery.

Inside, old Mrs. Whitman was asleep and snoring, daintily. Her son, Ted, was having a dream.

In the big room, Wendy Whitman was raging at her cousin.

"What do you mean by hanging around down here? Were you going to say a few well-chosen words against this marriage? Or maybe you thought you'd wait, for Ronnie to see how 'pretty' you look, in bed? Too old for me, is he? But just right for *you?* Is *that* it? You keep away from Ronnie Mungo."

Edie sat up and wiggled cautiously out from under the quilt. Her feet hit the floor and she stood up and moved toward the fireplace. Wendy turned and Wendy followed. Edie knew, now, that if only the boy kept quiet he was safe. It would cross nobody's mind that he could possibly be where he was. But she was afraid that Wendy might snatch at the quilt, Wendy might even launch herself at Edie, to scratch and bite. Wendy was in a towering rage.

"I'd be very glad to let Ronnie Mungo alone," Edie said, rather primly.

"*I'm* going to marry him," cried Wendy. She wasn't pretty now. She was quite frighteningly ugly. "Nobody's going to stop me."

Berserk? thought Edie. She remembered that she could always yell for the guard to come. She thought she would prod, she would attack, she would go on the offensive. Wendy was in a fit state to say too much.

"Tomorrow?" drawled Edie. "What *is* the big hurry?"

"Cousin Edie, remember what I said. . . ." Was Wendy struggling to control herself?

"So Myra tried to stop you last night?" said Edie. "What well-chosen words did she say? And what did you do about it?"

Wendy was visibly trembling. But she suddenly wrenched her body around as if she spun on the tip of one toe, and ran for the stairs. "Who listens to Myra?" she said, gutturally. "Or you? Or anybody so stupid?"

Wendy was going to run upstairs to her own room and it was best that she go. Yet, in the moment, Edie felt that she had failed and that she must try again. She had forgotten where the boy was. But she remembered the boy.

"Wendy." She stepped close to the stairs and looked up. "If you are running off tomorrow, won't you at least, before you go, admit that you might not have seen Harold Page?"

"Oh, what's the matter with you now?" wailed Wendy.

"Don't you know there isn't really any other evidence against him?" Then Edie could have eaten her words. What was she doing, trying to reason? With this enemy?

Wendy said, brutally contemptuous, "I'll say I saw him do it, then. I'll leave a note."

"Never mind. Go to bed." Edie bent her head. She dared not look behind her at the sofa. She had made another bad mistake. She ought to have let her cousin go.

She heard Wendy say, "Don't you tell me what to do."

Wendy had turned and was coming down.

"Let's skip the whole thing," said Edie, trying to smile. "I don't understand you."

"I'll say what I want." Wendy's voice was loud and it became louder. "And I'll do what I want. What"—

now she was screaming—"can't you understand about *that?*"

Edie took care to back away toward the fireplace. She was terrified, now. But she said, valiantly, "You don't care what you do to somebody else?"

"Hah, neither do you! You're the dopiest—If you weren't so busy fooling yourself, you'd know that *nobody* does." Wendy was not quite screaming but her voice was very loud. "Nobody gives one damn about anybody else, not really. Or ever has."

It seemed to tear out of her as if this were the truth, as Wendy saw it, and Edie gasped. "Look, that is . . . just not so," she said, with a pang that was almost pity.

"It *is* so." Wendy was screaming, again. Her face was flushed. Her neck was ugly. "It is *so*. Don't try to sell me your stupid ideas! They're lies!" Her head went back and the neck looked almost deformed. "Don't you think I know," said Wendy gutturally, almost strangling herself, "that Ronnie Mungo was *your* dream boat, when you were young? And you came back, looking for him. Hah!"

But Edie could not take this in. She was pierced now by alarm and enlightenment. "I wish I could help you."

She said it and did not think she would be heard but Wendy shouted, "You—do—not! Just remember! Ron is not for you. He's mine. Oh, I'm so *tired—*"

"What the devil," said Cousin Ted, irritably, "is the matter out here?"

Edie whirled. There he was, in his bathrobe, a brocaded garment with a satin sash. His back hair stood up. She whirled again. Wendy had backed up against the lower balusters and seemed to be plastered there. Edie didn't know what to do. She went sidling toward the sofa. She didn't know anything better to do than to slip into her corner, and hide her feet, and feel the presence of the boy. Her brain seemed to stop; the last image that faded from its screen was the remembered sight of the gun in Ted's pale hand.

When Mrs. Beck heard that raving, she bit her lips and began to trot. Just as she was, having just come in at the kitchen door, she hurried through the rooms.

She saw Wendy backed against the stair railing and her father crossing the carpet, sliding his feet, approaching her as he might approach a thornbush.

Wendy said, "Oh, go away . . . *everybody*. . . ."

Mrs. Beck heard the hysterical note. This would not do.

Her father said, "Sweetheart . . . Now, sweetheart . . . What's the trouble?" But he couldn't do anything with her, and he knew it. So did Mrs. Beck know it.

Wendy put her head back and shrieked. "Just . . . please . . . *everybody* . . . I don't *care*. . . ."

No, no, thought Mrs. Beck. Can't have *this*. She was in the big room now, and she put her purse and the paper napkin out of her hands, upon the top of the chest. She said to Mr. Whitman, who looked goggle-eyed in his helplessness, "I'll take her."

Wendy twisted and ducked away from her hand.

"Not a thing to worry you, my lamb," said Mrs. Beck softly.

The girl's bright eyes blazed. "I am not your lamb. I am *nobody's* lamb."

But Mrs. Beck could handle her. She summoned up her powers and began to do so.

Edie, twisted to look over the back of the sofa,

could see the housekeeper's black back, in that coat, but she could not see Wendy now, nor what Mrs. Beck was doing, with her right hand raised. She heard the house keeper begin to croon, "Who was the prettiest girl at the party? Who was the prettiest one?"

A sound came out of the girl; perhaps Wendy said 'No' but it was very weak.

"Come, love, Becky will take you up to bed and make you cozy and she'll fix some chocolate."

Now, Edie could tell that Mrs. Beck was touching Wendy's nape, stroking it softly with bare fingers. Wendy seemed to be almost falling. Suddenly, the housekeeper knelt on the floor. Edie could see Wendy's head hanging. Her hair had fallen over her brow. "Let Becky take your shoes, lamb? It was the shoes. Nasty shoes. Pinched you, didn't they?"

And Edie thought, appalled, She's talking to a child—a child of three!

Wendy answered, like a spoiled child of three, "I hate them." She kicked off one shoe. It slid on the carpet. Mrs. Beck made crooning noises and gently removed the other shoe. "We'll throw them away. That's what we'll do." She gathered up the other one.

"Throw them away," said Wendy. "I don't *want* them anymore." She was turning, docilely, as Mrs. Beck, now standing, was gently pressing her to turn.

"Come, lamb, come, love. Up we'll go, now."

They went up the stairs. Wendy went up in her stockinged feet, quietly, docilely, and Mrs. Beck went up beside her, touching her, stroking her. Edie had time to think, in wonder, Who is enslaved to whom?

Then Cousin Ted sighed, deeply. He walked in a small circle, sighing, "Oh, dear. Oh, dear." Then he glared at Edie. "*Why* do you cause such trouble in this house?"

Her mouth opened, and closed.

"What are you *doing* there, anyway?" he said, beginning to bluster. "It's after midnight. Go to your room."

"Yes, sir," said Edie meekly. She did not move.

"And try," the man blustered, "to be a little more considerate of your cousin, and all of us, in this very difficult . . ." He spotted the quilt and turned down his mouth as if he had tasted something rotten. "What is *this?*"

There was a loud knocking, somewhere. Edie's heart had leaped once, lurched, and leaped again.

"Oh, what now?" said Cousin Ted crossly, and he went trotting to the two steps, up them, across the foyer. Somebody was knocking loudly on the door.

Edie slipped all the way under the quilt herself, with one arm over the boy's shoulders, and breathed, "A little longer. We can't give up now. . . ."

He did not even move.

He didn't care too much, for himself, if it was now or later. He knew very well that he would be found. The floor was hard against his knees. He was perspiring. He noticed his discomfort. But it didn't matter, either.

He was thinking that once you had learned to suspect yourself, you did that first. Psyche and soma. Once you found out that your emotions could make you sick, you got into the habit. You blamed *them*. Like his foot. Plain old soma, but here he had walked on it, much too long and far, telling himself more than half of the way that it was mostly in his mind. Yes. He supposed that once you'd found out how some unknown part of you could make you do or feel what you didn't know you wanted to do, or feel—and it could just take you over—once you'd learned how to watch out for that, then you tended to blame *it* first, every time. Was that why he hadn't suspected? Kept blaming himself?

He was trying to figure out why it was that he had never thought, in all this time, that Wendy might have forces loose in her, and taking over, that *she* couldn't control. But now he could look back. Nobody had helped her. He hadn't helped her. He hadn't even known about such things in those days. Nobody had helped her at all. Not then. Not since?

He shuddered, then he tried not to shudder because of Edie, who was so scared and trying so hard to be kind to him. He realized that it would be better for Edie if he were not found now, here, where he was. For himself, it didn't matter. He would have to face up to it all, before long. To it all.

The guard was the same man who had been in the house during the afternoon. "I heard some screaming?" His air apologized.

"Ah." Cousin Ted was trying to recover the role of the master. "Shows you were alert. Good. But that was my daughter, poor little girl—very upset. Sensitive child. Her stepmother in the hospital and this wild man running loose. No sign of him?"

Edie, arranged against the arm of the sofa, half covered by the quilt again and ready to scream herself, thought, *I won't.* She beat down her need to scream. No, I will not. I will not turn this boy over to such a fool as Cousin Ted. And his gun.

She was suddenly brave and bold. Boldness was the safe way. "Cousin Ted?"

"What? What?" Cousin Ted wanted everything smooth now, so that he could go to bed.

"Would you please ask him to search my room? Because I'm afraid . . ."

"Nonsense," said Ted, with his usual confusion.

"Which is your room, miss?" the guard said, sounding happy to have something to do.

So she pointed, and the guard went cautiously up the lower flight, his gun drawn, with Cousin Ted, fussing and jittering, on his heels. The guard turned up the light in the turret room and both men went in.

Edie peeled back the quilt to let the boy breathe a moment's cooler air. "Don't move," she whispered. "*Sssh* . . . another minute, now. They . . ."

He turned his head and his face was flushed but composed. He whispered, "My shoes."

She swung the quilt back to cover him, knowing that he had remembered what she had forgotten, and wondering at the steadiness of his nerves.

Mrs. Beck came hurrying down the whole stairs, glancing in at the open door of the turret room on her way, but only briefly. She said to Edie, too absorbed in what she was doing to be surprised that Edie was there, "She's fine, now. It was just a little nerve-storm. Best leave her to herself, Miss Edith. I know what she needs. I understand her."

Mrs. Beck sailed off to the kitchen. Wendy was quiet, now. Looking at nothing. She was often so, after an outburst. Trancelike. And a good thing, too. Mrs. Beck would take care not to stir her up again tonight. But all was well. Mrs. Beck had come in good time. She took milk from the icebox, thinking, I've always been lucky.

Edie, waiting for what would come next, felt weary. But almost calm. They would find Harold's shoes, no doubt. But they would not find Harold. Not in the turret room, of course, and not where he was, either. There was something to be said for the set of their minds. They were so sure they were keeping him out.

The guard came down first and spoke to reassure her. "Nobody up there now, miss. I guess, though—"

But now Cousin Ted bounced out of her room, waving the shoes. "Look! Look!" He was beaming. "Edie, how was it that you didn't see these? No wonder you were frightened." He made no more sense than usual.

"Best to let Chief Tyler have those, sir," said the guard respectfully. And added, "They were under your bed, miss."

Edie was looking terrified enough, she felt sure.

"And here's proof!" Cousin Ted brandished the shoes, delighted with himself. "Oh, I'll keep them safe. And Charles shall have them, in the morning. He did get in by the tree. Well! I always thought so. I *said* so, don't you remember?"

The guard mumbled a 'Yes, sir,' although he remembered nothing of the sort.

"Now, you . . . you will keep your eyes open *and* your gun ready," Ted was admonishing.

The guard said stolidly, "Sure will, Mr. Whitman." He saluted and went up to the foyer. Cold air crept in from the wagging front door and touched Edie's cheek again.

Cousin Ted circled happily. "Well, I'm certainly glad that I had the foresight . . . Imagine, by the tree?" He stopped to look at her.

Was he going to ask her, again, how it had been possible that she hadn't seen those shoes? "The doctor phoned." Edie spoke quickly.

Ted was diverted. "Oh? Oh, dear . . ."

"Myra is in for surgery at six A.M. But Wendy said they don't think it is necessary for you to come down now."

That diverted him. He said earnestly, goggle-eyed, "They would know. They are the experts. I *am* ex-

100

hausted. I'll simply go down very early. Yes, that's wise. Oh, dear . . ."

His eyes darted this way and that. He wanted in the worst way to get back to his bed.

Edie said, as kindly and as warmly as she could, "You've had so much to worry you."

"Yes, I have," he said nobly. "Some rest, yes. You, too. Good night."

Edie watched him go. You get to be a liar in this house, she thought. You get to handling people.

She breathed long and free for a moment before she peeled the quilt away. The boy lifted himself up, stiffly. His face was flushed. Heat radiated from his body. The skin around his eyes looked bruised blue.

"Are you all right?" breathed Edie. "Oh, listen . . . never blame yourself for being afraid of Wendy."

"I know. I could hear. I'll . . . just go out and speak to the guard . . ." His foot failed him as he put weight on it. He managed to twist and fall, sitting . . . "in a minute."

She said, "I think you had better not. My room is safer than ever. Now, they have searched it."

"I can't hide like this anymore."

"I know it's not a very honest position," she babbled, "but we were lured into it, you might say, and now—"

"I can't, Edie."

"You'll have to, Harold," she said, severely.

He looked at her gravely, waiting to hear why.

"Because of the baby," she said. "Surely, you see that *you'll* have to get him away from Wendy, and them, and bring him up yourself?"

This was clear to her now. Very clear. Like a beacon. She wasn't analyzing, she just knew, that in all the hullabaloo, this was the guiding light. The true consideration. The justification and the far sight.

She watched his face as it softened to delight. "If I could . . ." She had touched a deep dream, a hope hidden.

"You don't dare not try," she said flatly. "So come on. And quickly."

He went with her up to the turret room. Edie turned off the light at the door, fearing too many shadows on a blind. She closed the door behind them and helped him, in the darkness, until the bed creaked under his weight. Edie sank to the floor beside him. She heard his throat clear to speak and she hushed him.

So he whispered, "Do you think it was Wendy? Do you think she had a . . . quarrel with Myra?"

"I know it," she whispered back. "I *have* known it. Oh, how do you know things? Tensions. Little looks. *I* was wondering . . . oh, long before you came. And I think Mrs. Beck knows it, too. Don't you?"

"But why"—he was gasping—"why don't the Whitmans begin to wonder?"

They were avoiding the mention of what might be wrong with Wendy, that ought to have been noticed.

"Oh, because their version suits them and they never change. Not if they can help it." Edie felt grim about this. "But—I don't see how to *prove* she did it, do you?"

"No."

"Well, she's not going to get away with blaming you," Edie whispered fiercely. "It's too much. I won't have it." She was as good as saying to him, it's not your business anymore. And it was not. It was Edie's business, because there was a child, and Edie knew these people.

"That woman is bad for Wendy. Oh, she is bad," Harold mourned.

"I know." Edie was not ready to think of Wendy as

102

a victim, of society or circumstance. "But I've known girls . . ." So-called "underprivileged" girls, Edie remembered, who had been physically and even mentally stunted by an environment. ". . . living in a world Wendy's never even heard of," she went on indignantly, "and doing better. Wendy's like a newborn. She always *has* been, Harold. Just as if she never did find out that other people can feel at all. Not that she doesn't care. She doesn't *know*. *I'm* afraid of her."

(But I'll beat her, Edie thought. Although not physically, I *will* beat her, this time.)

"You'll absolutely have to take that baby and you keep him and love him and teach him," she went on. "The courts are tough, though. It won't be easy. You have too many counts against you, already."

She could sense that he stiffened. "Berserk, and all, you mean?"

"And prejudice," she raced on, "in favor of the mother."

"I guess some men . . ." He was whispering on breath that moved both in and out. "I can't help it, about my baby . . . I do care."

Edie believed him. She didn't call it innocence or naïveté, but a kind of normal decency. A kind that could get you hurt, however.

"I've seen some women," she said, truthfully, "who don't care at all. Wendy doesn't want him."

"What *does* Wendy want?" She heard him murmuring, "I wish I . . . ever knew."

"Ssh. Listen to me. What if Myra, after the operation tomorrow, is able to say that it was Wendy? Then, you'll never be arrested for this trouble. There won't be that on your record, too. And neither will Wendy qualify to keep the baby anymore. Everything will be easier. So shouldn't we wait, and leave things as they are, a little while longer?"

Edie was arguing with somebody. She wasn't sure with whom. "I don't want the police to put you through some miserable inquisition, now," she went on. "You're not feeling well. It isn't fair. It isn't—wise, either."

"For the baby?"

(Yes, for the baby. For you, too. *I* care, thought Edie. Something, here, is all mixed up with what I *really* care about.)

"The only thing . . . you ought to see a doctor." Edie had begun to see that she was arguing with herself, and her conscience was stirring.

"Oh, that's nothing." He dismissed the state of his health.

"I know I'm busybodying," she burst out. "I just can't help it." She waited for him to dispute her arguments.

But he did not. "I understand about him being deaf, you know," the boy was whispering. He seemed far away, in a dream. "My father was a—you know—useful man and we loved him and my brother . . . It's nothing so terrible."

"I know."

"And I could take care of him."

"Yes." She groped to touch him and as she did, he went sagging down upon the pillow. "We must be quiet," she breathed.

"Yes."

Edie thought, Well, I won. Did I win? But I will win. And all I said is true.

She was wild to help him, now. She felt so fond of him, and such pity. And such partisanship. She thought he deserved his child and the poor little child deserved this father.

And Wendy deserved to be beaten.

She got to her feet, wondering what was to be

104

done, now, except wait for morning. She thought of the quilt, left behind them. She didn't want somebody helpfully bringing it to this door. She whispered her purpose to the boy and left him.

Everything seemed quiet in the Whitman house. There was no sound from upstairs, where Wendy had her nest. Edie flew down the lower flight, feeling lighter and freer, now that the boy was safe in the turret room. She wondered, briefly, about making another phone call, in the middle of the night, very urgently, to that Doctor Wesley. No. But she had glimpsed something there, on the chest where the phone was.

She went to look closer. It was a paper napkin. One that belonged to the house. There was the name on the corner, in that reddish brown. The Whitmans. She picked it up, to make sure, and a pin pricked her finger. Pins? Edie took the thing over to the end of the sofa into the lamplight. The paper napkin had been folded and pinned. Had someone been making a boat? Or a hat, for a child? What child?

She heard Mrs. Beck coming.

Edie put her hand down and the thing it held slipped between the soft folds of her peignoir. Mrs. Beck was coming from the kitchen, carrying a cup of chocolate. In order not to spill it, Mrs. Beck was staring at it, steadily. The housekeeper came, placing her feet carefully, straight into the big room and then on a curve to the stairs, and then she went—up, across the balcony, up the higher flight. She had not turned her eyes, even once. She had not spoken. She had not even seemed to notice Edie there.

Edie embraced the big puff of the quilt in both arms. She would wrap herself in it and sleep on a chair, on the floor, somewhere inside of her door where she could guard and yet be hidden. She was terrified.

Edie had heard of tunnel vision. That woman had a tunnel *mind,* she was thinking. She scampered up to hide, not understanding why, after such hairbreadth escapes, she was so frightened, now.

Wendy, in her ivory bed, would not, of course, *drink* the chocolate. Mrs. Beck knew that. Mrs. Beck would pretend to be hurt. After all Becky's trouble? No? Good night, then. Very hurt. But, of course, not really, because Wendy had to hurt *her* sometimes. Mrs. Beck understood that very well.

Conrad, on guard, stood in the moonlight and looked up at the tree. Sure, it could be done. He could do it himself. Swing hand-over-hand along that one big branch and you'd come right to the window. Your feet would hit the sill, just right, with enough spring left in your knees, and then you could take ahold. He could see where. A casement window. Say it was open? Easy as pie. Or even if it wasn't open. Then, would this nut have taken off his shoes? Might. Some of these lunatics were pretty sly, or thought they were. The guard looked behind him at the darkest thicket. No wind. If a leaf moved, you'd know it, on a night like this.

Harold Page did not move. He lay quietly, living the whole thing — with a difference — over again.

It had been a bloody night in the small seaside city. Cars had moved, unluckily. A drunk had run head-on

106

into a carload of merry widows. A man had had a flat and stopped too close to a curve. A sports car had glanced off his rear and rolled over into the path of a bus. Sirens had haunted the distances.

At the hospital, speakers had called out doctors' names. People had run in the corridors. But now, late, the town settled.

Myra Whitman did not move.

As if she had been hit on the head, Edith Thompson fell a thousand miles into sleep, on the floor of the turret room.

The guards on the outside of the Whitman house shuffled their feet; they yawned.

The moon moved and went down; the sun came up.

Chapter Eight

Mrs. Beck was never tired. She was up and bathed and attired in a spotless fresh uniform, ready for what the day would bring. It had brought nothing, yet. Well, too early, she supposed. She crossed the big room to open the draperies, noting that there was dust in here. Well, Angie would be back on Saturday, which was tomorrow, and maybe Selma, too, so Mrs. Beck would give it a lick and a promise later on. *Maybe,* she thought.

She peered out to see whether the guard was there, wondering about breakfast for three of them. She would wait for orders. Probably there would be no such orders.

Mr. Whitman said, behind her, "At his post, is he?"

"Oh yes, sir. He is there." Mrs. Beck turned her head and gasped. Mr. Whitman had a gun in his right hand. He was fully dressed for the day, in his dapper fashion, and his small feet in their shining shoes trotted firmly.

"Oh, this," he said. "I'll scarcely need it at the hospital, mad as he is." Mr. Whitman was making for the chest under the balcony, to put the little gun away.

Mrs. Beck said, agreeably, "No, sir. I'll have your breakfast, sir. Coffee is made but I hadn't expected . . . You are early, sir."

As he lifted his hand, Mrs. Beck caught a glimpse of motion and saw Wendy coming down the stairs. She was in her blue pajamas and her short peach-colored quilted robe. Mr. Whitman was saying, "No, no. No breakfast. They may have Mrs. Whitman on the operating table right now. I must get on. It wouldn't do. After all, there *is* a coffee shop." Now he looked up and saw Wendy on the balcony.

He shut the top drawer and looked at his wrist.

"Has my watch *stopped?*"

"Ronnie's coming," Wendy said.

"This early!" Her father goggled.

"Maybe."

Mrs. Beck, listening carefully, widened her lower lip and felt her chin flatten. She willed Wendy to look at her. Wendy glanced at her and said, "I don't want too much, Becky, but I want it now."

"I'll fix breakfast right away, Miss Wendy," said Mrs. Beck, in soft submission. She went around Mr. Whitman and into the dining room. She went no farther.

"I don't understand," Mr. Whitman was saying. "Oh. You are coming to the hospital?" (Mrs. Beck rolled her eyes, he would never learn.)

Wendy said bluntly, "What for?"

"Oh. I thought perhaps you were going to stand by . . . Of course, it isn't necessary, sweetheart. If it would upset you. Well . . ."

(Mrs. Beck could almost hear the slow turn of his brain.)

"But why is Ronnie coming so early?" he exclaimed.

(Mrs. Beck listened hard for this answer.)

"Maybe we'll get our blood tested." Then Wendy added impatiently, "so that we can get a marriage license, Daddy."

"But there's no hurry about that, surely. Myra won't

be out of the hospital, at the very best, for some time yet."

"I know. But we could have a 'little' wedding or a 'quiet' wedding. Or something."

(Mrs. Beck jerked up her chin. Oh no, she thought. Oh no, you don't!)

Mr. Whitman was talking. "Sweetheart, mind you — I have *not* said that you *may not* marry Ronnie Mungo."

"That's good. Because I'm of age, now. And you can't say it." It was sullen and there was latent anger and Mrs. Beck took a step.

"But I *must* say," Mr. Whitman was going on, "that both Myra and I were very much surprised by your announcement and we feel that this man, while he is of good family and has money—"

(Oh no, groaned Mrs. Beck to herself, he will never learn how to handle her. He will always make a mess of it.) She was not at all surprised to hear Wendy's jeering voice cut in, *"Had* money."

"No, no, but as Myra says, he *is* older, he has had so much experience . . ."

"Myra," said Wendy mockingly, "should be careful what she says."

Mrs. Beck stepped briskly into the big room.

"Now, please." Mr. Whitman was turning around, walking in a little circle in the way he had of doing when he didn't know *what* to do. "Let us not . . . I haven't the time," he said.

Wendy said, "I'm not asking for any of your time."

"Well . . . tell Ronnie that I want to talk to him." Mr. Whitman was starting for the foyer.

"Why should he talk to you?" Wendy called after him. *"I* don't even have to talk to you."

She was spoiling to quarrel with somebody and Mrs. Beck guessed who would do. She walked farther into the room, smiling and nodding.

Mr. Whitman saw her and was relieved. "Now I must go," he said fussily (as if it mattered where he went or when). "Now I must be off. Now, I *am* late. I hope you won't do anything too . . ." His eyes were asking Mrs. Beck to take care.

"That's all right, sir," she said to him reassuringly.

He went away, reassured. Leaving things to her. Where they belonged.

Wendy stood lacing her fingers and looking at them. Mrs. Beck said, "Honey lamb . . ."

But she wouldn't look. She went skipping to the telephone. "If Ronnie is going to be here, he won't be *there*."

Mrs. Beck went after her. "There is no hurry," she crooned. "There really is *no* hurry. I told you—"

"Oh, be quiet!" Wendy tossed her head and her eyes flashed defiance. "He should have left—"

Then the phone rang, under her hand.

Mrs. Beck took three steps backwards, folded her hands, and waited quietly.

In the hospital, when they had found her, they had made some gestures, in the interest of opening the way for a miracle. But they had expected none, and none came. Myra was not to be resurrected. In the midst of this activity, however, a nurse had discovered the little scrap of torn pliofilm and now came grave and secret conferences among the staff. It was not until almost six in the morning that Dr. Sturdevant, Myra's physician, asked whether the family had been notified.

It turned out to be his duty to notify them. Someone else would call the police.

By the time the good doctor reached a telephone, he had missed Theodore Whitman, the daughter told him. Mr. Whitman was on his way to the hospital now. So the doctor told Wendy that he had some very sad news, that Mrs. Whitman had died during the night, that he knew this must be a great shock—

Wendy cut in on him. "Well, thank you, I guess," she said in a voice that was both tense and forlorn.

When she hung up, he let it go. He went down to the lobby to wait for the husband.

Wendy hung up and looked at Mrs. Beck and the housekeeper looked deep into the brilliant eyes to see what might be stirring. She said softly, "I told you." She thought she could read in the eyes that Wendy had not taken her meaning, until now. Ah, Mrs. Beck had thought not. But now, surely, Wendy would see that all was well and there was no need to do anything precipitously.

Edith Thompson startled them by calling down from the balcony, "Was that for me?"

Wendy said "No" sharply and turned her back. "It was nothing."

"Was it the hospital?"

"Miss Wendy said it was nothing, Miss Edith," said Mrs. Beck reprovingly.

Edie came running down the stairs. "How could it be nothing?" she challenged.

"A wrong number is nothing," said Mrs. Beck, haughtily. Then she said to Wendy, "Come, lamb. Have your breakfast?"

Wendy did not want to come. "I was going to make a phone call."

Mrs. Beck did not want to go. "Miss Edith?" She suggested where Edie should go. "Will you have breakfast?"

"Oh, Becky," said Wendy, almost gaily, "don't *fuss!*"

So their eyes met and one of Wendy's brows flew up and Mrs. Beck thought, *That's all right.* Still she did not want to leave these two together. Everything had to be watched, everything. And listened to. So the house-keeper drew apart, but she did not go.

The one sound that penetrated to the turret room was the shrilling of the telephone. Edie had been sure it was Dr. Wesley, calling back. She had been ready. Dressed in her cheap green-and-white cotton check, and the little green flat slippers she had found, for two dollars, and wore so proudly, she had been brushing her hair.

The boy sat in a chair because, he said, to lie on the bed too long was tiresome. His foot was better. Edie thought he seemed listless, but his fever was, at least, no worse. He was patiently waiting.

Edie herself felt bold and strong this morning be-cause, by her watch, Myra was already being prepared for the surgery that was going to make her able to tell the saving truth. It was a question of waiting patiently. Edie knew that it might be hours yet. She must smug-gle him some food.

They were talking. They had developed a muted way of speaking that was better than a whisper.

"I've got it figured out, you know," said Edie. "That is, *if* you said in your letter that you might come here."

"I said I wanted to see the baby. I said I *could* come."

"That's a part of it, then. But listen. You were noti-fied that the divorce was final? Then, Wendy must have been notified at the same time. All right — that's why she announced her engagement on Sunday."

Edie stopped the motion of the hairbrush. Was it?

"She's hell-bent to marry Ronnie Mungo," Edie kept on, aloud. "I don't understand her. Or him, either. She — told me that money was the thing."

"Money?" The boy straightened and he looked as bewildered as she had felt by such a thing.

Edie began to pull the brush slowly through her

blond mane. As soon as Wendy was free to marry, Wendy had announced her engagement. That was on Sunday. On Sunday evening, her cousin Edith Thompson had arrived. Had Wendy, perhaps, wanted Ronnie Mungo openly committed to her before Edie appeared? No, surely that couldn't have been a factor.

But it was true that Ronnie Mungo had been what Wendy so sneeringly called Edie's "dream boat" ever since the day that he had chosen her, out of a bevy of young girls, giggling and squealing at the tennis matches. The day he had taken her into the clubhouse for what? A lemonade! Memory made her squirm. He had asked her for a date, Ronnie Mungo, the rich, the charming, the older-man. But nothing had ever come of it. She had been forced to break the date. (Wendy had seen to that.) He had seemed to take this lightly, had never called her again. Edie had wept more than one night. As Wendy knew. But Wendy couldn't have been afraid . . .

The boy was saying, "Something bugging you, Edie?"

He was leaning back and for the first time she saw him as he must have been before Wendy Whitman had chosen him to destroy. Nice-looking, easygoing, physically attractive, full of good humor, cheerful and slangy. Aware no doubt of the counter-moral world that boys know, in which to go to bed and walk away was the thing to do and as often as possible. But a boy who, for all of that, had taken his marriage seriously and no doubt more seriously than he had seemed to take it.

Now, Edie guessed, what appeared to be his naïveté was candor. Having had to pick up the pieces of himself, he had put them back together differently. He had been trained out of the normal ways that the young have, of covering their feelings over with such thick

114

layers of currently fashionable slang phrases that the sentiments often sounded like their own opposites. She knew how kids talked. It was a part of her job to probe through to the loneliness, the panic, or even the human yearning to be good, that they hid from the whole world, and often from themselves. But this boy had been probed and in the process stripped.

"What's up?" he said now.

She smiled at him. "Personal tangent. Where was I? Oh yes. About Ronnie Mungo. Wendy hasn't been dating him very long. The family was surprised at the engagement. Nobody said a word against it, of course, because what Wendy wants, little Wendy gets. But now I'm pretty sure that Myra must have been the exception. Well, if she did say a few 'well-chosen words' on Wednesday night, Wendy is perfectly capable of flying into a fit. She's not used to being denied. So they fought, and Myra fell, and out she conked. It had nothing to do with you at all."

"I guess not," he said quietly.

"But, now hear this. Wendy or Mrs. Beck or both of them knew what was in your letter. So they used it. They simply fitted you in. They didn't care what happened to you. They wanted Charles Tyler to waste his time and keep away from Wendy. Because *he* was furious."

It made Edie furious. It made her sick. The callous ruthlessness.

"And then, you see, you walked right in," she said.

"I wonder why I came?"

Edie's mouth opened.

"I said it was to find out about the baby. And it was. Truly. Partly. I also thought that since I was going to school, and going for a . . . well, a career, I guess you'd say . . . I ought to face them first and face them down. By 'them,' I guess I was meaning Wendy. I wanted to show her that I was still alive, and okay, and going places. But it isn't any use, you know, Edie. I would just like to get out of here, now."

She understood him. "Sure, and *I* guess *I* came," she told him, "to show them that I was somebody, all by myself. But they are not impressed." She whacked at her head. "Why should I care so much whether they notice me or not? That's what I'm wondering, now."

"It sure looks like you're the last to know why you do what you do."

She looked at him sharply. He was slumped in the chair, not necessarily directing his remark at anyone.

All right, Edie admitted to herself. Wendy almost got it right. I came to lay a ghost. Here I am, being courted . . . by two men, in fact . . . Simon Carr. Good, kind, gentle, long-suffering, and very like my father. The other one, Tony Lynch, is poor, but lively, and is not going to be poor forever. He couldn't care less about the poor, as such. Although he is absentmindedly moderately generous. So what is my problem? I won't know until I lay the ghost of Ronnie Mungo, and all that phantom fun, the rich and easygoing good times, the glamour and the leisure I never got to try and never will. With Tony, I'll work until he makes it, and *then* what will I do with myself? It'll be late, for glamour. With Simon, I'll work until I die. Will it have a meaning? I don't know. I don't know. How dear to my heart is . . . anything? I don't seem to be in love. But was I? Once? With Ronnie Mungo?

When the phone rang, she had thought at once, there's Dr. Wesley. She had waited for Harold to move, lest he be seen through the opening door. Then she had rushed forth.

When they said the call had not been for her, Edie believed them. The thing to do was to wait, as quietly as could be, until her call did come. She had intended

116

to go meekly to her breakfast and watch her chance to steal a meal for Harold Page. But there was Wendy, looking very pretty, tousled as she was, standing with her hand on the telephone. *I am expecting an important call,* thought Edie with a stab of irrational anger. She said, "Are you feeling better now?"

Wendy's head snapped around on the neck as if she'd been severely shocked. "What do you *mean,* better now?"

"Better than you did last night?" said Edie, with mild surprise at so violent a reaction.

"Oh, *why!*" Wendy cast Edie out of her attention and picked up the instrument.

"Because," said Edie, moving closer, insisting upon attention, "I'd like to ask you, now that you are calmer, whether you are really going to stick to that lie about Harold Page."

"Oh," burst Wendy, *"what* lie?" She pushed her hair out of her eyes. "I wish you'd stop nagging and nagging at me. Will you please?"

Edie heard the housekeeper say, in a warning tone, "Miss Edith . . ."

But she moved around to be able to see Wendy's face. Wendy was dialing. "You may cause trouble," Edie said, "but you'll never *prove* he did it. And if you tell that lie in a courtroom, there is a law —"

"Oh, *law!*" Wendy whipped around to turn her back.

"No law for you?" said Edie, in cold fury. "Then why should you be afraid to tell the truth? Nothing can touch *you,* can it?"

"That's *right,* Cousin Edie," said Wendy looking over her shoulder, with her mouth tucked up at the corner. Then she ducked her head and her hair fell forward.

Edie heard the housekeeper, behind her. "I

think . . ."

Wendy tossed her head high. "He doesn't answer. He must be on his way." She was smiling.

"All you are thinking about," said Edie, "is marrying Ronnie Mungo—come hell or high water?"

"Right, *again*." Wendy's brow flew up. She was triumphant. She stretched like a cat.

"And you won't even listen to me?"

"Miss Edith, I don't think . . ."

"Why should I listen to you?" said Wendy cheerfully. "Why is this any of your business?"

"Why is what any of whose business?" said Granny, briskly. "Good morning."

There she was, dressed as Lila Whitman would be dressed even at this hour, quite elegantly, in blue. She had tiny blue earrings on, very tiny "morning" earrings. Her small person was tidy and perfumed.

The group of three broke open. Wendy danced away. Mrs. Beck moved toward the dining room, with a submissive duck of her head. Edie said to Granny, "You're very early."

"*Too* early," Granny agreed. "For the simple reason that I went to bed too early, and enough is enough. What are you talking about so early?" Her blue eyes darted from one girl to the other. Wendy was mum. She scarcely seemed to have heard the question.

"Why," drawled Edie, "about Wendy eloping with Ronnie Mungo today."

"Don't *you* love to cause trouble!" cried Wendy, throwing her head back but keeping her eyes almost closed. It was as if there was something here she did not want to see. Edie glanced behind her and saw the tall white figure of the housekeeper seeming especially tall, especially rigid.

"Really, Wendy," said Granny in her own lofty manner, "what are you thinking of? With Myra in the hospital, being cut up this very minute, or so Ted tells me," Granny was in full flow, "it is very bad taste to run away and marry anybody. As for Ronnie Mungo, what is *he* thinking of? I wonder."

Wendy laughed. Her eyes flashed open. She was filled with reckless elation. "Oh, he's been lying awake, all night, thinking about the money."

"Whose money?" said Granny, suspiciously.

"*My* money. I looked it up, Granny." Wendy was insolent. "My mother's money. You can't do anything. Nobody can. Not now."

Granny's eyes, for once, steadied and she gazed coldly at her granddaughter. "We shall see," she said.

"Yes, won't we?" Wendy taunted her.

"My poor child," said Granny, and Edie was surprised to hear the genuine pity in her voice, a condescending pity from one who felt herself superior—yet pity. "I have no intention," said Granny grandly, "of wasting my energies trying to make *you* see what *I* see. Especially at this hour, and without my coffee." Pity had vanished.

"Coffee is ready, Mrs. Whitman," said Mrs. Beck obsequiously. "Miss Edith."

As Granny started to cross the room, Mrs. Beck said to her, in a different voice, in an aside. "Better let me handle her."

Granny stopped and slowly turned her elegant head. Her whole small elegant self proclaimed that this was her kingdom. Mrs. Beck had overstepped. Granny said, with a faint fastidious lifting of her pink lip, "I think you will find, Mrs. Beck, that, on the whole, everyone tends to go to hell in her own way, and there is no use bothering about it." Then Granny, stepping rather high, walked proudly out of the room.

Mrs. Beck went swiftly to Wendy and touched the girl's nape but Wendy twisted away. Staring, fascinated, Edie stood still until she realized that the house-keeper was sending *her* a steady stare, was watching Edie watch, was making a cold and hostile suggestion. Go away.

Edie said, "Excuse me." She started for the dining room, to snatch at the opportunity she could see. Then she thought of something else. "Wendy, if Ron is coming for you then you won't need your car?"

"Why?" said Wendy, sullenly.

"May I borrow it, please?"

"No," said Wendy.

"Why not?"

"Because I don't happen to feel like lending you my car, Cousin Edie."

Edie could tell that Wendy was simply being difficult, for no reason to do with Edie or the car, but just to be difficult. It was intolerable.

"So that is the law?" said Edie in silky fury. "If you don't feel like it, then you don't do it? And vice versa?"

"Well, bully for you," said Wendy. "Right, three times in one day!" She darted around Mrs. Beck to the bottom of the stairs. "I feel like getting dressed," she said airily.

Mrs. Beck came striding toward Edie and she said, with her brows drawn together in a kind of aching sweetness, her voice purring, "Miss Edith, wouldn't it be best if you didn't argue? The automobile, after all, is Miss Wendy's property."

Edie said sweetly, "Of course. She may do as she likes . . . with the automobile."

She went swinging furiously through the dining room, the pantry, into the big kitchen, to the breakfast room that was only partly partitioned off. Granny was sitting there, very stiff and upright in her chair.

"May I bring you some coffee?" Edie tried to swallow down the signs of her anger.

"Not at all," said Granny. "We hire a servant."

So Edie, behind her back, filled a cup and found a sweet roll to put on the saucer. It was all she dared to take. She put the meager breakfast well to the back of a shelf in the pantry, to be smuggled up to Harold Page as her chance arose.

She was thinking, Money? Wendy *is* marrying for money. Her own money, which she gets when she marries. But she didn't get it when she married Harold Page, having been too young at that time. Didn't she know that she was too young, as stipulated in the will? Was money the meaning of *that* marriage—to Wendy?

As Edie poured coffee for herself, Granny said, "As long as I have exactly what I require for my comfort, Mrs. Beck may run this house. But not *unless*. Will you go and tell her, please, Edie, that I wish my breakfast served at once, and I wish my toast well buttered?"

And Edie thought, This matters. *This* matters. Not only that she be served, but *who* serves her. She thought, How terrible!

In the big room, Mrs. Beck said, "You mustn't run away today, lamb."

Wendy, who had been motionless on the third stair, backed from the banister to the wall and then circled downward. She avoided the woman and danced free in the room. "What do you mean, I *mustn't?* It's if I *can,* Becky. If Ron gets here in time. And I get *away.* Before they find out . . ."

"That Myra is dead?" said Mrs. Beck softly. She took a tiny step. "Why, I told you. I said there wasn't any hurry. And there isn't. Not now, lamb. Oh, I knew that you were worried. Lamb, I knew. But nothing is going to happen. They'll blame the madman. So you needn't run away and miss"—Mrs. Beck was near

121

enough to touch her now — "all the pretty clothes," she crooned, "and the presents and the parties and the flowers and the champagne . . ."

Wendy pushed her hair back with a nervous hand. Mrs. Beck could tell by the change in her eyes that someone was there. Edie called out, "Excuse me, Mrs. Beck? Mrs. Whitman would like her breakfast served and her toast buttered."

"Yes, miss," said Mrs. Beck. "Right away." Her mouth contorted. *"I'll butter it,"* she growled in her throat when Edie was gone. She bent to the girl. "Come, lamb, think about your lovely wedding and the whole town to see you in your beautiful gown. And then when you go to Paris, or some happy place, Becky will be along to take care of you and fix your hair. And always take care of you."

Wendy, still under the woman's touch, went slowly to the sofa and put one knee on it. Then she collapsed, she let herself fall on the soft face down. She lay quiet.

Mrs. Beck moved around behind the sofa, and looked down. The mop of hair was over the brow. The breathing was quiet. The hand she could see was re-laxed and limp, where it lay. Mrs. Beck nodded and went swiftly, almost on tiptoe, away.

She'd have to butter up the old lady, for now. It wouldn't do to have a run-in with *her.* Not yet, thought Mrs. Beck with satisfaction. But one of these days.

As for Wendy, poor little lamb, she would be all right. This was all too much for her, so hard . . . But Mrs. Beck could take care of her. And always would. And always, always would. Mrs. Beck would run the wedding.

She passed Edie in the pantry. This Edith was a nui-sance, but she didn't count for much else, surely.

* * *

122

Edie was carrying the cup of coffee and she fixed her gaze on it, so as not to spill. She had good balance and her legs were lithe to obey her so that she walked fast. She sped through the big empty room. (Wendy must have gone, she thought, on upstairs to dress.) She was halfway, when the turret room door began to open, and by some peripheral sense, Edie knew it. She stopped and looked up.

"Go back!" she warned, low in her throat. "Don't be seen!"

But he stepped out upon the balcony. Oh, dangerous! "Was it Dr. Wesley on the phone?" he said.

"Oh, no, no, not yet. Oh, listen, be careful." Edie gazed on the coffee and hurried. It sloshed a little as she went up the stairs.

"He *will* call," she said to him, earnestly, as they met on the balcony. "This is for you. Oh, please . . ."

The cup and saucer went from her hands to his and the liquid sloshed over the rim. "I'm nervous, Harold," Edie said, surprising herself. "I don't know . . . I just sense . . . Come. Eat. Aren't you hungry?"

He lurched on his bad foot, turning, going back into the turret room. Without looking behind, Edie closed the door.

Down in the big room, Wendy was lifted up, on the sofa, like a lizard supported by its forefeet. Strands of hair fell over her eyes, but not so many that she had not seen.

Chapter Nine

The old lady was demanding, very demanding, picky and choosy about every single thing. But Mrs. Beck was humble and strong to endure. Finally the meal was over and the old lady was left with her extra cup of coffee and the morning newspaper, which she seemed to enjoy. She habitually read every line on the society pages, and never made a comment.

Mrs. Beck felt free, at last, to scurry back into the big room.

Wendy was lying on her face, on the sofa.

"Now, lamb," crooned Mrs. Beck, "you see? Wasn't Becky right, lamb? Now, you should come and take your breakfast. And make our fine Mr. Ronnie Mungo wait a little bit?"

Wendy lifted up like a lizard, and said hoarsely, "*What* did you tell me last night?"

"I said there was no need to worry. Didn't I say that, lamb?"

Wendy got to her knees. "What . . . did you do?"

Poor lamb. Afraid? "*Sssh*," Mrs. Beck gave warning.

"Oh, I . . . You see my white uniform?" She had been very clever, very resourceful, and it was pleasant to explain. "And I made me a little nurse's cap, out of a white paper napkin." She hadn't been able to find that napkin, this morning, in this room. No matter. It belonged in the house. "Nobody stopped me," she crooned. "They won't know. They'll blame the mad-man."

She had been very very careful. She had had to wait a long time, in the hospital, for a safe chance. But she had taken care to arrive after Mr. Whitman would have left. She had hidden her dark coat and had felt forced to go check on it, every now and then, to be sure that no one had put it helpfully elsewhere. She had walked in the corridors, testing her disguise. Carefully. No one had questioned her. But it had taken a long time for her chance to come. Not easy, to have been so patient and careful.

But around midnight, there had been a lot of excitement. By that time, the corridors were quite dim, and when everyone was suddenly so busy, then Mrs. Beck had slipped along and into Miss Myra's room.

It had been too bad, in a way. Miss Myra had not looked as if she would ever say anything. But if she did, then a long dream died and Mrs. Beck knew how to save it, surely and carefully, and put an end to worry. It was simple, although chancy for a short time, of course. They had left Myra's door propped open and Mrs. Beck had not dared to close it all the way. But she had dared to put the thing over Myra's head and step into a shadow and wait. That was all it took. She had been a *little* nervous, waiting—and afterwards, tearing at it with her nails, to split it and get it off. But she had done it. Quick and easy, once she had wisely waited for her chance.

Then she had found her coat and walked four blocks to a bus, shredding the pliofilm bag as she went and getting rid of pieces. No one had questioned her. Noticed her, even. How smoothly she had done it! No one could possibly know.

"Even if they figure out what happened to her, they'll just blame the madman," she soothed. (Why not?)

But Wendy jumped up and whispered hoarsely to her face, "You are a fool! You are stupid!"

"Sssh. No, no. You forget. Myra could have wakened up and said it was you, lamb. We didn't want that."

"Stupid old fool!" wailed Wendy.

Mrs. Beck sighed inwardly and began her pursuit. She took tiny steps. She crept nearer. "Ah, now . . . Ah, now . . ." But Wendy stopped her own tiny steps away, and tipped her head suddenly to gaze at Mrs. Beck with those brilliant frightened eyes. Defiant?

Mrs. Beck thought she had better let her have it. Good and strong. "You think Myra wouldn't have told? But oh, my lamb, remember, it wasn't as if she had just fallen. Oh, she fell. But then you were on her, like a wildcat, and banging her head and crying and carrying on . . . I saw it. I heard it."

Let the girl remember how Becky had taken her out of that. "Your daddy would have to do something about you," she added softly, "if I told them."

The girl bent, as if her spine snapped. "She shouldn't have said that I was bad."

Mrs. Beck was nodding, approvingly.

"And put on that act about an 'old friend she was so fond of' "—Wendy was mocking viciously—"and not wanting *him* to get mixed up with *me*. The hypocrite!"

"Ssh. Sssh. I know. Her and Mr. Mungo." Mrs. Beck licked her lips. "*I* told you that, when she first came."

And so she had. She did it to turn the girl against Miss Myra. In those days, Mrs. Beck had been afraid of Myra. So, a nasty secret, to be kept "for Daddy's sake." But Wendy blocked from ever being won over to Myra, no matter what blandishments the strange woman in the house might have tried. (In Mrs. Beck's domain.) It had been a way to handle Wendy, all right. *Then*. But Mrs. Beck took fleeting note of the fact that Wendy had grown. "For Daddy's sake" would never work. Not now.

"She shouldn't have said," Wendy whimpered, "that I was lost and I was impossible."

"Now, lamb, don't get yourself excited. It's all over. There is no need. Becky's got you out of the whole thing. Nobody will know."

Mrs. Beck put out her hand, but Wendy ducked and skipped away. "I'm getting myself out of it," she said. "I'm going with Ronnie. As soon as he comes. As fast as I can. Today."

Mrs. Beck had overstepped, somehow. She knew it at once. She sucked her lip. She said quietly, "Where?"

"To Mexico. And then to Paris. And then around the whole world—anywhere, away from here. Away from this whole mess. And away from you, too."

Well, Wendy had to hurt her sometimes, but only in unimportant ways. This would not do. Mrs. Beck said, "Mr. Mungo promised me—"

"I don't care what he promised. *I* don't want you anymore."

All was not well—anymore. *Nothing* was well. My life, thought Mrs. Beck. My whole life! "Oh, but you can't leave me here, Miss Wendy, lamb! I'm not going to be stuck here with the old lady."

"I'm going to dress." The girl ducked around her and ran to the stairs. So? She would do what *she* wanted, when *she* wanted? So *she* thought? You little fool, thought Mrs. Beck. *I live your life.*

"You may as well not bother," she said coldly. She wasn't crooning. Wendy stopped and looked. "When they find out, they'll make you see the doctors. When they find out," said Mrs. Beck, taking tiny steps, approaching, "that it was you who knocked your stepmother down and beat her head on the hearth, like a crazy girl."

But Wendy leaned over the banister and sent down a ferocious whisper. "Then, they'll find out that it was *you* who did something to her in the hospital—so that she died."

Mrs. Beck took a tiny step backwards. Wendy turned like a tiger and came sneaking down and around the newel post.

"They won't—notice," said Mrs. Beck. "It was her head—"

"Yes, they will notice." Wendy was approaching. Mrs. Beck stepped back once more. "You are an ignorant old woman. Besides, *I* can always tell them, can't I?"

"Come, lamb," said Mrs. Beck. She licked her lips. The lamb was a sudden lion. "Ah now, come, love. We'll have to put it on the madman, the both of us. What's the harm in that?" she wheedled.

"You're a fool! What you don't know . . . Harold is right here in this house. So how could he be in the hospital last night? You don't know everything."

"I don't believe you," said Mrs. Beck. (But she was startled.) "In this house!"

"That's right and you'll be in for it, but *I'm* not going to be, Becky."

"I don't believe it," said Mrs. Beck again.

"Don't, then," the girl said. "I don't care. But they'll know whatever it was that happened in the hospital. And *I'm* not going to be in the mess you're in."

They knew, in the hospital, what had happened. Charles Tyler was there and he knew. Murder. Someone, with malice aforethought, had got in here and killed his sister Myra. Not in sudden passion, but carefully, by patient plan.

Tyler ran a small department. He was himself the head of Homicide. He could leave the meticulous examination of the hospital room to his expert and the routine questioning of everyone on the floor to a plainclothesman, the sharpest detective that he had. By phone, he mobilized his uniformed men to beat the bushes all over town.

A kook could have some lucid moments. Or hours. It had to be the one who had beat her up in the first place. Or if not, Charles Tyler would know the reason why. Get that kook! *Get* him! Flush him out of the bushes. Get him to *me!*

Ted Whitman he had left, temporarily, to the doctor, who was comforting him with pills and platitudes. Somebody would have to drive the poor wretch home. Tyler, Tyler supposed. He had to go there anyhow.

Mrs. Beck's eyes were turning sideways, slyly. "What if they do know, at the hospital, how it was done? The madman still did it. He got in here afterwards. That's easy."

"No, it's not," said Wendy. "How could he get in here, during the night, with the guards all around? You're stupid!"

But Mrs. Beck had thought of something. "No. The guard on the front was *inside*, one little while. I saw him. I remember. So that's what we can say.

129

That's when somebody . . . Miss Edie must have let him in."

"Oh, she . . . did . . . that!" spat Wendy.

"Well, then, *she's* in for it," said Mrs. Beck, feeling briefly encouraged. "We'll put it on her and the madman. I'll tell you what to say, lamb. Don't you worry. Becky will always be nearby."

Mrs. Beck was thinking, Let her take some tranquilizers. Let her play she's upset, "for Myra's sake." Put her to bed, and I'll watch. Mrs. Beck was trying to believe that all was well, but it was not. She had made a stupid mistake just now. She needn't have said a word. There was no use appealing to Wendy, "for Becky's sake." Wendy had grown out of all that sort of thing. Mrs. Beck had to get Wendy in hand. Then she could deal with the rest of it.

Wendy was looking at her under lazy eyelids. "Becky, I — don't like this much."

"No." Mrs. Beck had to agree. With the madman in the house, everything was touchy and chancy. That Edith could be a real nuisance. It was very upsetting.

"But you know," said Wendy, "we *could*. I saw where Daddy put his gun."

Mrs. Beck was startled. She looked suspiciously at the girl. What did she mean? Did she mean what Mrs. Beck thought she meant? Well? The housekeeper checked over the house, in her mind, rapidly. The old lady should be safe in the breakfast room for a good while, yet. Mr. Whitman was gone. Where was that Edith? She said, slowly, "We would be afraid . . . just women . . . of a madman *in* the house."

Wendy turned on her toe and glided to the big carved chest. She opened the top drawer, reached in, and her hand came out with the little gun. "It's loaded. He didn't bother."

Oh, now wait, thought Mrs. Beck, in a fluster.

Now, wait. . . . She hurried to Wendy, who held out the weapon. Wendy's hand was shaking.

It came to Mrs. Beck that this "mess" could be mutual, and perfectly so, even as they both got out of it. In her mind basked the long dream. Wendy, in possession of her own fortune, and Mrs. Beck, alone, to groom her and advise her. And that Ronnie Mungo (whose fortune had diminished and who was therefore vulnerable) to be their gigolo. Until, if *he* got to be too much of a nuisance, Mrs. Beck could always break up the marriage. She had done it before. Then, she might find a nobleman for Wendy, perhaps. Whatever turned up, that seemed desirable. The dream was long. And glorious.

But Wendy must be brought to hand, *now*. Mrs. Beck must make their positions clear, if she wished to partake of the full glory of the dream. She thought she saw the way. What about a kind of stalemate?

She said, "It won't make any difference, which of us . . . Remember? That's the law." If Wendy knew that, that was one thing.

"I know. I know that." The girl's hand shook. "But I'm too n-nervous." The gun was about to fall and Mrs. Beck snatched it. Her hand was not shaking.

Still, she did not quite know how this was to be done. It wasn't a bad idea, thought Mrs. Beck, all by itself—to get rid of the madman. Since then they could say whatever they liked about him, and a dead madman would please everybody and relax all nervous vigilance. If, at the same time, she could entangle Wendy consciously in a conspiracy to kill . . . Mrs. Beck did not put it quite that baldly to herself. It wasn't a bad idea, she thought, because Wendy was an excellent liar, providing she was lying "for Wendy's sake." Mrs. Beck, who was already a murderess, saw nothing to lose. But one must be careful, of course.

The housekeeper backed away to look up at the turret room. "What about that Edith? If he's with her . . ." How could it be done, in that event, at all?

Wendy said, throatily, "Oh, he's not up there. He's in the cellar."

"How do you know?" snapped Mrs. Beck. She walked around to where the cellar door was cut in the turret wall. The key was in the lock. "It's locked," she said.

"I know. I locked it."

"*You* did?" Mrs. Beck looked at her sharply, but Wendy was swaying a little, as if she were exhausted by all these problems.

"I thought I heard something," Wendy said drearily. "I just cracked the door. I don't think he saw me."

Mrs. Beck did not quite believe her. She tended to doubt that the man was in the house at all. Maybe Wendy was having hallucinations. (This was possible.) She held the gun in her left hand and turned the key with her right. She felt the girl's breath. She felt (and she shivered) Wendy's fingers on the back of her neck.

"Becky, it's silly to be afraid of him, isn't it?"

Mrs. Beck was more than physically touched. Why, Wendy was scared—and just a baby, really! Mrs. Beck had to look out for them both. She felt the girl's fingers as an appeal. For just a moment, she almost believed in love. "I don't know, lamb," she murmured.

Wendy said, "But he didn't do anything, really—did he? *I* knocked Myra down. *You* killed her. *Didn't* you, Becky?"

Love fled. Mrs. Beck twisted her neck and gazed into the brilliant, reckless, threatening, hate-filled eyes.

"Unless we put it on the madman," Wendy said,

"how are we going to get out of it?"

"This will be the both of us," said the housekeeper, sourly.

"I know."

(Wendy was willing? She didn't beware of putting herself in the worst of the mess, too? But *was* there any madman to do it to? Mrs. Beck felt confused.)

"There isn't much time," Wendy was saying softly. "Ron should be almost here. Of course, I couldn't run away with him today, could I? I mean, if . . ."

Mrs. Beck felt suddenly fierce and righteous. She firmed her hand on the doorknob. "If the madman is in our cellar," she said, "he has *no business* there." She yanked open the door. The only thing in her mind was, I'll have to see. I'll have to see.

Then she felt the force on her back, the flat hand pushing, violently. She tried, too late, to catch her footing, but the cellar stairs were steep and went almost directly down. She felt the first shock, as her shoulder hit the stone of a step, and the second, as her arm bent wrong. And then, in pain, she tumbled on. She felt no shock at all, from the hard stone floor.

In the big room, Wendy turned the key and put it in her pocket and went dancing away from the closed and silent cellar door. Screaming at the top of her lungs.

When Edie popped out of the turret room, Wendy was standing down there, still in her robe, with her hands to her head, screaming and screaming. One couldn't hear another thing in the world!

"What's the *matter?*" Edie shouted.

Whether or not Wendy heard, she answered, in a lesser scream, "Somebody! Somebody in the tree! The *tree!*"

Edie ran down the lower flight and looked out and

up, at the tree. She was frightened. She felt as if her hair were turning white and her scalp knew it. But the tree stood, as it always had—huge, grotesquely near—an uncanny tree.

Now, she heard Granny. "Oh, mercy! Oh, my heart!"

So Edie turned and raced across to the old lady, who was tottering near the dining room door. Granny was frightened, too.

Edie said to Wendy crossly, "There is nobody in the tree. For heaven's sakes!"

Wendy was still, suddenly, with her arms tight at her sides, looking as if she had almost been frightened to death, thought Edie.

Now, Granny was babbling piteously. "The tree? Don't let me see him. I do not wish to see him." She was holding her thin-boned delicate hand over her eyes.

Edie guided her to a chair and sat her down. Then she ran to the place near the bottom of the stairs where the cord hung, grasped it, and made the velvet slide. The room darkened. Almost all of the tree vanished from sight. Only a leafy portion hung motionlessly above the velvet, against the sky.

"Wendy, what is the matter with you?" blazed Edie. "Nobody's there. Couldn't be. The guard's right outside. And he's going to be in here any minute, thinking somebody's been *murdered!*

Wendy was very pale and she stared. Her whole body was shaking. "I'm sorry," she stammered. "I'm nervous."

Granny said, "You have certainly made *me* nervous."

"But I thought . . . There was a shadow. Like a big . . . a s-spider. Look, I'm just shaking."

She certainly was. But Edie could feel no sympathy. "Go find Mrs. Beck," she said rudely. "She'll comfort you. *I'd* better go tell the guard it was all in your mind."

Edie ran up to the foyer and out the front door. (Ah, but the air was good!) The guard already had his gun drawn and was coming around the corner. Edie breathed in deep and sighed out, and began to explain.

Granny was saying, in a voice like tin, clanking, "You are very inconsiderate, Wendy, to have nerves at your age. And I don't think you are in any condition . . . Where are you?"

"Here." Wendy's voice was faint and feeble. She was somewhere back, near the cellar door.

". . . in any condition to make any decisions whatsoever. I shall sit here and not budge. If this Mungo boy appears, I intend to speak to him. Perhaps you will not elope today."

"Won't I?" Wendy sounded distrait. "Oh. Well . . . There isn't any . . . hurry." She was drifting across to the stairs. "But I'll dress," she said with sudden firmness. Then her voice cracked, shrilly, "In case, you know?"

Wendy ran up the stairs as fast as she could run. She flew into her room and shut the door. She began to snatch and assemble the elements of a costume, but in a moment she dropped everything, fell on the bed, face down, and put her hands over her ears, although — from the whole house beyond her door — no sound could reach her.

When Edie came in and saw no Wendy, but only Granny in her chair, she ran in a panic up to the turret room and fearfully slipped within. The boy was alone, standing at the side of the eastern window, looking downward. He turned and came to her, quickly.

"Just Wendy, having a fit of some kind," Edie panted.

"I heard you, outside." He put his hand under her elbow. "You didn't tell the guard about me?"

She shook her head. "I promised you . . ."

He neither praised nor reproached her. His hand was hot and dry and strong. "You all right?"

She nodded. She asked him, silently, to wait, and silently he nodded that he would. So Edie left him, thinking that he was the coolest, sanest single person in this terrible house. Imprisoned here.

Harold was feeling sane enough — but hot and weak and sad, and he sure wished he could get out of this.

Edie pulled herself together and sauntered down to the big room. Oh, this staircase and the door to the turret room, suspended halfway, in full view . . . the last possible exit. But hold. Hold on. The good news could come soon.

She said to Granny, trying to make light of Wendy's hysteria, "What was *that* all about?"

The old lady stopped the kneading motion of her thin pink lips and spoke sharply. "I do not know. I certainly do wish that they would catch this madman and be rid of him. It is simply too nerve-wracking." The phone rang. "Answer that, Edie, please. I cannot budge."

Chapter Ten

At the first note of Cousin Ted's voice, Edie thought, with a wonderful surge of relief, He knows! It's all over. Myra has told them who did it. But when the voice went on, in that tone of frenzied grief, Edie felt stunned. She seemed to be making the proper responses, of shock, of sorrow, of concern for him. When he choked and hung up, she went to Granny, still feeling numb, but duty bound to break the news.

Granny said she assumed the news was bad and what was it?

"Myra has died." Edie softened her voice as best she could but she had no softer words.

The old lady's brows went up. She began to fumble with the little box on her breast, as if to suspect it. "What's that?"

"Oh, Granny, she was already dead when Cousin Ted got there."

"On the operating table?" asked Granny loudly and calmly.

"No, no. In her bed. Cousin Ted said they tried everything. But . . . I am so sorry. For her. For everyone."

"Then she was murdered," said Granny, in the same bold voice. *"My* son's wife."

"What did you say?" Edie had been thinking—if anything—that Myra could never speak, would never tell, and for this she had been so stunned and sorry. Now she took it further.

"Murdered!" said Granny vehemently. "And in this house. Right there." She pointed. "Right there. It may be in the newspapers." The old lady balled her dainty fist and struck the chair arm. "Oh, what is to be *done* about this madman! Call Charles Tyler at once."

"Mr. Tyler is with Cousin Ted. They are coming here. I don't know what to . . ." Edie straightened from where she was bent over Granny. She looked up at the turret room. Her heart felt like a small hard stone. Myra was dead of her injuries. Harold Page was wanted for murder now.

At the hospital, Cousin Ted mopped his eyes pitifully. "I simply couldn't go on."

"Just as well," said Charles Tyler. "They'll hear *how* it happened, soon enough." He, who had questions to ask, didn't mind the advantage of a bit held back.

"That's what *I* thought," said Cousin Ted, expanding with anybody's approval, "much better to break it in stages. My mother, you know . . . my poor mother. And Wendy . . . so sensitive. I should sue, Charles, I think. Really. In a hospital? If people are not safe in a hospital . . ."

Tyler said, "I'd better get you on home. I have work to do. We'll go now." He was in charge.

What to do? thought Edie. She could think of absolutely nothing that she could do.

"I must have a yellow pill." Granny was fumbling

138

with a tiny silver pillbox. Her voice had faltered from that bold calm. She was nearly whimpering. "I am all thumbs this morning. Open my box, Edie. I can't open my box."

Edie took the tiny thing in her hands, but her fingers were cold and stiff. "I can't, either," she admitted.

"I don't," said Granny, stiffening and summoning up some strength for her voice, "I don't *propose* to carry on about this. Ted will, of course. It is expected of him."

Edie felt as if she had been slapped in the face. This was so monstrously cynical. Or was it?

"And Wendy will carry on when *she* hears," said Granny, grimly.

"I ought to tell her." Edie winced at the thought.

"Oh, *ought,*" said Granny. "A little peace. A little minute." The blue eyes were darting to and fro. "Myra was a cold woman. I never wished her any *harm*. It is very cold in here, Edie. This was always a cold room. Perhaps it is the tree. Fetch me my white wool shawl—somebody? Where is Mrs. Beck? I have some yellow pills on my dressing table, I do believe."

The old lady was trying to struggle to her feet. Edie caught hold of her arm to help her, as the phone rang. They stood a moment. It rang again.

"I shall have to cancel my luncheon on Saturday," said Granny. "If that is for me, I *cannot* speak now."

She seemed to have her balance, so Edie went to the phone. "Mrs. Beck?" she called in the direction of the dining room and kitchen. There was no response. The phone kept ringing. Edie picked it up.

"Miss Edith Thompson, please?"

"Yes, this is she . . ."

"Dr. Wesley calling."

"Please hold on, just one second." Edie put her

139

hand over the mouthpiece. "It's for me, Granny." (At last. At the wrong time. But at last.)

"I cannot speak on the telephone now," said Granny regally. "I must have a pill and my white shawl. I don't know why it should be so cold in August." She was proceeding, walking slowly but fairly steadily, toward the east wing, mumbling to herself. "Weather is not what it used to be. Seasons are all confused. Myra was young and I am old."

When she was gone, Edie let her breath out. "Hello? Dr. Wesley?"

"I believe you asked me to call you?" said a man's voice.

"Yes, sir, I did. I am related to the Whitman family. This is about Harold Page."

"Oh, yes?"

"Dr. Wesley, I may have to speak fast." Edie looked on all sides while she talked. Mrs. Beck would appear any moment, surely. Or Wendy might come downstairs.

"A terrible thing has happened. Someone got in here, at the Whitman house, on Wednesday night, and injured Mrs. Whitman who was taken to a hospital in a coma and has now died." Edie felt proud of that sentence. It was pretty good. It told a lot. "All of them here," she hurried on, "think it was Harold Page, and the police want him."

"Harold left *us* on Monday . . ."

"I know. But he didn't do it. He *is* here now. I have him hidden."

"I beg your pardon? *Hidden,* did you say?"

"That's what I said." Edie was forced to swallow.

"You are speaking from the Whitman *house?* He is *there,* you said? They don't know it?"

"No, they don't know." Her sentences were sounding sillier. She didn't know how to frame another.

"I am wondering," the voice said suavely, "why you called *me?*"

"Well, could you come down, sir, and help me? Help *him?* He didn't do it."

"My dear Miss Thompson," the doctor said, "surely you can tell the police that he didn't do it. In what way . . . why should *I* come?"

"Why because, although it isn't true, his ex-wife is swearing that she *saw* him that night."

"I should think that it's a matter for the police, really."

"Yes, but surely *you* must see how it is the same thing, all over again."

"The boy is all right, you know."

"But to go through . . ."

"I see. *I* see." The voice was enlightened. "You think that he will be damaged emotionally; perhaps you are thinking 'psychologically'? But Harold is perfectly well, you know."

"He *isn't* well, physically. He has a fever."

"Then he ought to see a physician."

"Yes, sir, I know that."

Edie wanted to grind her teeth. She began to think there was such a thing as being *too* sane. She couldn't seem to reach this man with any of her own sense of tragedy and peril.

"I think," he was saying now, "that you mean to be kind. But Harold Page is as able as any of us to meet whatever his environment presents, and he ought not to have special privilege. He is not a cripple, Miss Thompson, and he need not lean or depend."

"Yes, I realize . . ."

"So we mustn't treat him like a cripple, must we? Don't you agree?"

"Yes, but isn't there anything?"

"I doubt that there is any wise thing that I can do.

141

You say he is unjustly suspected of a murder? The police will surely investigate, will they not?"

"Yes, well . . ."

"I would say that you ought to *call* the police, at once. To have hidden him is — unacceptable behavior and I, frankly, am rather surprised that Harold allowed it. He knows he must face reality." The doctor suddenly stopped sounding stuffy. "Turn him in, my dear," he said. "Trust the authorities. Secrets and stratagems are pretty romantic."

Edie said coolly, "Thank you very much for your advice."

She hung up. She thought, I'll get the guard. No, I'll tell Harold. No, *first,* I'll get the guard. No, I promised. She seemed to hear the front doorbell clear its throat. She sped up to the foyer to throw the door open. She would fling herself upon Charles Tyler.

Ronnie Mungo said cheerfully, "Good morning."

Edie stepped backward and let him in. "You are so wrong," she said into his smiling face. "This is going to be one of the worst mornings I ever saw."

"What's up?" He looked alert.

"Oh, listen . . ." Well, fling herself upon anybody. "Could *you* do anything?" she cried.

Ron took her by the arm and helped her down the two steps. He glanced around and saw that they were quite alone. "How can I say," he answered in his lighthearted way, "until I know what the matter is?"

Edie pulled away from his hand. "No. No use. Wendy will lie and lie and lie . . ." She sunk her teeth hard into her forefinger.

Ron said, unperturbed, "What about? And where is she?"

"She's dressing, I guess. To run off to Mexico with you. Or so *she* imagines." Edie didn't care what she said anymore. She couldn't think what to do.

"Imagines?" he drawled.

"Myra is dead." She threw it at him.

"Oh, oh," said Ron softly. "Well, that does put the frost on. Too bad. I was fond of Myra—in a way." The pleasant smile-wrinkles framed, she saw, a pair of foxy eyes. "Were you?" he asked, obviously wondering why *she* should be this much upset.

"You don't know the half of it," Edie burst out. "Harold Page is in my room."

"What? You don't mean the 'madman'?" He wasn't taking it seriously yet. He was putting quotes around the noun.

"Only he isn't. He didn't *do* it. He wasn't *here* that night. He hasn't done one single thing that's wrong. I've had him hidden in my room since yesterday."

Ron took her by the shoulders with firm hands. He was looking down at her with a stern expression. "For God's sake! Why?"

"Because I couldn't get him out," she cried. "Cousin Ted has had us bottled up. And now Harold's own doctor tells me what a fool I am. So *you* needn't bother."

"I wasn't going to," Ron said. He smiled at her, now, but she sensed that wheels whirred in his head.

Edie began to mimic the doctor's voice. "Harold Page is 'as well able as any of us to meet what his environment presents.' So, the poor kid, sick with a fever, walks right into a murder charge. Oh, I've done well!"

"Murder?" There was an edge to the pleasant voice now. A shock?

"Well, of course, murder!" she cried. "He is supposed to have knocked Myra down and broken her head and now she is dead of it."

Edie was feeling as isolated as if she lived in an iceberg, all by herself. Was she the only one in the world who cared what happened to Harold Page? "And I have to go and tell him." She hid her face.

In a moment she heard Ron's voice, close to her ear. "You mean to say this chap is innocent?"

"Yes. Yes. Yes. Even of being mad. But it won't *matter.*" She turned her back.

"You're sounding pretty upset, Cousin Edie."

"Oh, *I've* been a romantic idiot," she wept. "I haven't 'faced reality.' And now the jig is up. The bubble's burst. The end has come."

She had no handkerchief. She mopped her face with her sleeve. Then Ron was putting his handkerchief into her hand. "But look," he said with a certain comical stubbornness, "if he didn't *do* it, then he *didn't* do it? Did he?"

He had almost made her laugh.

"Maybe I don't get all this," Ron said.

You don't, she thought, but you may as well have it. Her heart jumped as she said quietly, "Are you wondering who did?"

Her vision had been mopped clear and she looked directly at him. What kind of a man was this, anyway? If she had laid the ghost, killed the dream she had once built up around him, then she did not know him at all. She did not know why he had come, so early in the morning, to run away with Wendy because Wendy insisted. A man who had had two wives already — could he have built a romantic dream around Wendy, aged nineteen? Or was it Wendy's money?

He said, "Oh, come on now, Cousin Edie, I know Wendy takes a bit of handling. Are you calling her a murderess?"

Had he read her mind or had he thought of this before? No matter. No difference. Edie said, "All right. I can't prove it. But Myra is just as dead."

She turned her back on him and walked away, trying to compose herself and make ready to go up to the turret room and tell Harold Page what was up. Poor Myra, she thought. I haven't spared her a minute, to mourn her.

But she hadn't known Myra, either.

"I don't see," said Ron, "what you thought you were going to do with him."

She turned around and he was looking a little angry, which was odd.

"Get him away, of course," she cried. "Out of this house and out of this town. Where the Chief of Police is the victim's *brother,* and that's a darling situation, too." She was going to cry again. She sank into a chair and huddled there, using his handkerchief.

"Edie, maybe *you* had better calm down."

She had to agree with that. Oh yes. Be calm. Don't care, that meant. Stop caring. "What does it matter," she raved, "if *I* rant and rave like Wendy? Anybody might as well. I couldn't help him. I can't, now. Oh, the world has moved and left *me* far behind. I was trying to be . . . I don't know what . . . to do good, I guess. But it was only busybodying."

She realized that he was crouching beside her, that he seemed about to pet her and comfort her. That would be intolerable. Edie pulled herself straight and took one hard swipe at her eyes with the handkerchief. "Okay," she said sternly. "So much for me. Oh, he'll be all right. That is, if they don't shoot him on sight. That is, if they have enough pity to get him to a doctor before they beat him with sticks, or something. *Maybe* he won't suffer too much. *Maybe* he won't get sent back, as a homicidal maniac. Somebody else might believe him. It *may* come out that Wendy drove him there in the first place, with her lies, and doesn't mind if she does it again. Justice

145

may prevail. If it doesn't, then Wendy will just get away with murder. Two of them. Myra. And Harold Page—to all intents and purposes. That's wrong, *I* think. Flat wrong, plain and simple. That is, if anything is simple anymore."

Ron stirred and said, "Er . . . could I do anything?"

"What could you do?" Edie flashed. "I forgot. You came to carry Wendy off and marry her."

"Could be," he drawled, "I suddenly don't feel like marrying Wendy Whitman."

"Just because she's insane?" Edie then became ashamed of herself. She got out of the chair. Jumped into her familiar skin. "I'm very sorry, Ron," she said in her normal voice. "Pay no attention to that, please? I don't know what to *do,* you see. There's nothing I can do about this."

But she found herself feeling a little better. It was dead-end, frustration alley. You snarled and you bit. But after a while, when you were sane again, you just hit the wall. She could not help Harold Page.

So she had been insulting a stranger, this Ronnie Mungo whom she did not know, because a dream or two had died—but *he* had not dreamed them. She said again, "I'm sorry. I shouldn't insult you. You have nothing to do with it."

He was looking at her thoughtfully. There seemed to be a tiny worry line on his brow. "I'm sorry, too," he said, "because it looks to me as if *you've* had a little too much to do with it. Aren't you going to be in a bad spot?"

"Oh—" Edie dismissed that.

"Look, I guess I see why you did all this. But I don't think Tyler is going to take it kindly. Matter of fact, I think it's against the law."

She shook her head sadly.

"Not going down too well with the old lady, either. Is it?"

"No," said Edie, who didn't care about that.

"Do you know what I think? I think we had better get him out of here."

Chapter Eleven

"What?" Edie didn't trust her ears.

"Right now." (He meant it?)

"How could . . ."

"I have a car out there."

"There's a guard out there," she said, bewildered.

"Then get him in here."

"How?"

"Call him in. Tell him a story. Tell him you're hearing sinister noises, somewhere inside the house. Get him out of *this* room, and the way is clear."

"Would he come?" Her heart beat faster.

"What's he there for?" Ron held his head tilted. He was grinning at her. His eyes were reckless.

"Then you'd take Harold?" She couldn't believe it.

"Certainly. Whisk him out of town. That's what you would like. That would take you off the spot."

She said, in confusion, "I want *him* back where he'll have somebody on his side, *some* chance." But that was wrong. Dr. Wesley wasn't on Harold's side. Oh nonsense, of course he was—although not romantically.

"There's going to be one hell of an uproar if he's caught in *your* room," said Ron rapidly. "You're going to land right in the soup. Harboring a wanted man."

"He's not a murderer."

"I believe you. So—get him out. Chicken?"

"Are you doing this for me?" She couldn't imagine why he was doing it.

"For auld lang syne," Ron said lightly.

"There wasn't any."

"Then for the auld lang syne that never was," he said. "You're pretty cute, Edie."

"Don't tease me."

"For kicks, then," he said impatiently. "Call it that. Shall we *do* it?"

Now, she saw a thousand reasons why they couldn't do it. "Cousin Ted and Mr. Tyler are on their way—"

"They're not here, *yet.*"

"But will he go?" She started for the stairs.

"Well," said Ron with a great shrug, "if he won't go . . . that's gratitude for you."

"Is there *time?*"

He came over to her and spoke rapidly, making a plan. "You call the guard. Right now. I'll lure him where we want him. You put your pseudo-madman in the back of my car. Make him lie low, on the floor. I'll nip out and drive off. Why not?"

She thought, Does he think it's a game? Then she thought, Yet why not? The way things are is so bad, so dangerous, so wrong. What way could be any worse than the way things are?

Ron said, "Aw, come on, Edie. Just as I'm finding out that do-gooding can be fun."

She couldn't help but smile. "Where shall I say, though?" She ran up to the foyer. She was thinking of Granny, Mrs. Beck, Wendy. "There are people all over the house." East wing, west wing, upstairs. "I'll have to say I'm hearing noises in the cellar."

"Cellar. Fine. That'll do. Quick, now."

Edie knew they had not thought this through. But

149

there wasn't time to think it through. There was only just time enough to do it. Surely, it would be better to get Harold Page out of the house. How could that be doubted, whether you could produce your reasons in an orderly row or not?

She was out in the air again, in the bright morning. The guard saw her at once and turned toward her. She ran to him; he was still Conrad, the one she knew. "Oh, could you please?" Edie made herself breathless, which wasn't difficult. "There *is* somebody in the house, I think. There's something making noises. Now, we're all scared."

"Inside!" But he was moving. He would come. "Where, miss?"

"In the cellar. Something *down* there . . ."

"I'll take a look." He followed her.

They hurried across the tile of the foyer and down into the room, so darkened by the drawn draperies. Coming in from the sunshine, the guard was blinking.

"It seems to be a kind of rustling," Edie was improvising.

"How could he get in there?" the guard muttered. "I locked the outside cellar door myself." He was bristling now. He stopped short, as Ron met him. "Sir?" He blinked.

"Better check, don't you think?" said Ron, in a low voice, as if not to frighten the intruder. *"You'll* know how to handle it."

"Yeah. Sure," the guard said. "I can handle it."

He walked and Ron, beside him, became a kind of guide. They were going around the curve of the wall. At the cellar door, they would be invisible from the stairs. The stairs would be invisible to them. Edie was poised to ascend.

Then she heard Granny's voice. "Who is that man? Young man?"

Edie looked and there sat Granny, in a chair near the door to the east wing, wrapped in her white shawl, looking as if she had been sitting there for hours.

"Oh, Granny, go away!" wailed Edie.

Ronnie Mungo had said much the same, although more tactfully. "Mrs. Whitman, maybe you had best not be out here just now."

But Granny, trotting into the big room, with her shawl wrapped around her snugly, had gone on talking to herself. ". . . help remembering how one lies down in one's coffin. I do not believe that this is the time to . . . I believe that I would rather sit . . . How do you do?"

Then she had sat down, established herself. "Ronnie Mungo, is it not?" the old lady had said. And then, "There has been a death in the family."

When Edie, poised on the first step, wailed in disappointment, the guard took it for female fright. "It's all right, ladies," he said to her and Granny, too. "I can handle it." He said to Ron, "Could be a rat, you know. Something of the sort. This is the cellar door, right?"

Ron said, in a voice too loud, "Get him out."

Edie knew that he spoke to her. All right, she thought, do it anyway. In spite of Granny. She won't know what is happening soon enough to stop it. Edie ran up to the balcony. No, no, she thought. If Granny sees him, she will cry out, and the guard will look. He might even shoot.

The guard was not looking, now. He had taken Ron's words as addressed to himself. "Listen," he said, "if he is down there, I'll get him out, all right."

Granny shrilled, "Get whom? You are in *my* house."

151

"Get the madman, ma'am." Conrad accepted her authority.

Granny's voice began to tremble. "In the tree?" she quavered. "The tree? I have never really been comfortable with that tree. . . ." She was remembering the fright that Wendy had given her. Her thin hand came to cover her eyes. Edie saw Ron swing to the old lady. He was going to stand over her, distract her, keep *her* from looking. She heard him say, "The tree?" Too loud. To Edie?

Well, of course. *The Tree!* Edie nodded understanding. The draperies had been drawn. Lucky! Harold could swing out of the turret room by the route of the tree limb. Could do, in reverse, what they were all so sure he had done, were afraid that he might do. The guard, at least, could not see any part of the big window from where he was, near the cellar door.

But the guard was not near the cellar door. Edie heard his call and looked down. He was directly below her, looking up. "Where is the key to the cellar door, miss?"

Ron said, "I'll find it. Can you hear him, down there, now?"

Ron veered away from Granny to shepherd the guard back around the curve of the wall. Edie, on her toes on the balcony, her hand sweating on the knob of the door to the turret room, heard a sound she was not making. Latch click?

Ron had reappeared below and was gazing up. Everything was frozen—except the front door of the Whitman house, which was swinging open.

Edie said, in a false bright voice, with the ridiculous inflections of some ancient stage-piece, "Here come Cousin Ted and Mr. Tyler now!"

"Find the key," called Ronnie Mungo. "If you can. Maybe you can. The tree?"

Nobody noticed that he had not said "key" a second time. Except Edie, who thought, Nothing could be worse than it is — so why not? They'll be distracted, too. This is better.

"If I can," she promised gaily.

Cousin Ted was entering slowly, as became a man bent under a great sorrow. Before he and Charles Tyler had come down into the big room, Edie had turned the knob and slipped from their sight.

She had to explain to Harold very quickly. She had to get him to move, to go, to understand — very quickly.

He had heard the phone ring, a couple of times, but Edie hadn't come. He had heard her speaking to the guard again, just now. Outside. He hadn't caught it all. He'd heard the word "cellar" so he knew she hadn't been mentioning where he was. He was alerted, though. Something was up. So when she came, on such a wave of urgency, he was ready to listen closely.

"The guard's inside. Everybody's there. You've got to get out, by this window. By the limb of the tree. Slide down the trunk. Can you do it, Harold? There's a red car, parked near the front door. Scrunch down and don't let the other guard see you. Get into the back seat and lie on the floor. Quickly. Right away. Ronnie Mungo's going to drive off with you. You have got to get out."

He was making a kind of token hesitation. He was going to do it. He'd be glad to. Right away. But she added, "Myra is dead. Now, they think you murdered her. I know you didn't. Do this for me?"

It shook him. It really shook him up. He turned, under her pushing hands, and by the strength of his own first impulse. Then he was crouching in the narrow embrasure. His bad foot held him well enough. The window was slightly open. He pulled it open all the way. There was no guard below. Not far above his head was the limb of the tree, in easy reach. He glanced at the big window below. The draperies were closed. He wondered if Wendy was standing the other side of them. If he thought *once more* of Wendy, he couldn't do it. And he wanted to get out.

The limb of the tree was very thick. He must cup his hands well over the top of it. It wouldn't do to fall. He would break his foot again, or a leg. If his arms didn't feel so heavy, in themselves, if he wasn't feeling so rotten, lousy, altogether, it would be a piece of cake. But he could *do* it.

The girl was saying behind him, "Quick. Quick. Quick."

So there was no time to think whether he should.

Ted Whitman reached the floor of the big room just as his mother screamed, a tiny, dainty "Oh," but a scream, even so.

"What?" said Ted. "What?"

Mungo was there and he said, "There's someone in the cellar." Old Mrs. Whitman, from her chair, was hanging to his sleeve.

Charles Tyler pushed past, saying with relish, "That so?"

And the old lady said in a shrill quaver, "Now, Teddy, don't *you* get killed. Let somebody else go."

"Oh, Mother . . ." said Ted.

Edie, cracking the door of the turret room, heard Cousin Ted saying, "Myra . . . Mother, did they tell you?"

And Ron say to him sharply, "The cellar, sir. The cellar." So Cousin Ted was turned and directed toward the cellar door.

"Now is the time," said Ronnie loudly, "to be a brave girl."

Edie was past being brave. Harold was already launching himself upon the tree. She could not help him. She might, by helping Ronnie get away. She started down.

The guard said from around the curve, "No key, sir."

Tyler said, "Where *is* the key?"

She saw that Ron was gazing high above her head. She knew that the glass was bare, high in the pointed arch. She knew that the leaves of the big tree would be shaking, there.

No one else must look. No one else must see. What could they do with Cousin Ted, who hadn't gone far enough, who wasn't out of the way yet. *He* might see.

"Cousin Ted, you must have a key to the cellar door," Edie sang out.

So Cousin Ted began to pull his key case out of his pocket. "What? Key? To the cellar? Why yes. Naturally, I have a key."

So he went, in almost his normal gait, around the curve to where the other two men were standing. From there, none of them could see the window or the shaking of the tree.

Edie found herself clinging to the newel post, not daring to look behind and above her.

Granny, grasping Ronnie's sleeve with a tight little hand, was bridling and babbling. "I am neither brave *nor* a girl, young man, but it is kind of you. What *I* shall do is sit. I can't help thinking that if one were to die in any sudden public way, one's limbs . . ."

The tree limb shook. The eastern sun was shifting southerly. Edie could see the shadows. Leaves were dancing on the carpet, over there. Over there.

". . . may be tumbled about and one's clothing disarranged . . ." Granny went on and on ". . . and one might look perfectly vulgar and unable to do a thing about it. And after a long life, during which one has struggled to behave with decorum, at least . . ."

Edie let go of the newel post and raced to Ron's side, where he was trying to disengage the old woman's clutch upon his sleeve. Edie must take over here. Ron had to get out of the house too. And into his car, in order to drive away. Quickly.

She could see the group of three now, around the curved wall, near the cellar door. The guard said, "I guess you gimme the wrong one, Mr. Whitman."

Cousin Ted said, "What? Oh, dear . . ."

And Tyler said, "Get *on* with it."

Granny tightened her fingers and said, "Ronnie Mungo? There was something I was going to say to you. But this is *not* the time . . ."

"No, no," said Edie. "Let *me* . . ." She put her hand on Granny's little claw and began to work, to loosen those fingers.

"When I was young," said Granny, "there were so many strong young men. Where are they now?"

"*Sssh,* Granny . . . let me . . ."

Tyler said, warningly, "Stand away, Ted."

The guard must have found a key that worked and he must have turned it. Ted stumbled backward.

And the tree shook. The shadows danced on one bright patch of carpet. The leaves were dancing against the high glass. A twig scratched? It scratched on Edie's ear like a scream.

But the two men, Tyler and the guard, had their guns out and they stood concentrated and waiting upon the exact right second to open the cellar door. It's going to work, thought Edie. It'll be all right.

156

We'll *do* it.

Ronnie Mungo moved his arm abruptly and tore the sleeve of his jacket out of the old lady's grasp. Edie was bent to take over here, to stand by the old lady. He was turned toward the window. He could go, now. Ron's left arm came up and his hand fell upon her shoulder.

She knew it fell, signifying doom. She looked behind her. Wendy was coming down the stairs. She was wearing a summer suit in peacock blue, with a turtlenecked white blouse. Her head was bare. She was lugging her small white train case. She was stepping to the balcony. Her tiny pretty feet twinkled in bright blue.

Edie could feel the old lady's hand like a nest of trembling wire, she could feel Ron's hand heavy and warm and ominous on her shoulder. The shadowed leaves made a dancing pattern, all around the three of them, that Wendy could not help but see.

Oh, Wendy, let him go.

But Wendy, staring downward, had seen the dancing shadows. Slowly, she turned her head. "There is somebody in the tree," she said promptly, loudly, but with an air of perfect calm, and no hysterics whatsoever.

"What? What's that, sweetheart?" Cousin Ted stepped back still farther. Now he could see.

"He is getting out, Daddy," said Wendy, in that same matter-of-fact manner. "By the tree. See?"

Tyler came quickly to Ted's side. "Stand still."

Now, Charles Tyler could see.

Granny said, "Is it the wind?" Granny had seen.

The guard, with his gun drawn, came to where he could see.

See the leaves shake, unnaturally, in no wind, and shake one last time and then seem to be trembling to stillness.

Edie was between them all and the window without

157

knowing how. "No," she was saying.

She heard her cousin Wendy say, in a note of exasperation, "Why is it that you never believe a word I say?"

Then, Wendy ran down to the cord, yanked it and the draperies opened.

Harold Page, in his white coat, with no shoes on, was pasted against the base of the huge trunk, not clinging but limply leaning. As they watched, his foot went from under him, his body began to slide. Slowly be slid and he crumpled. He melted into a silent heap on the ground.

Chapter Twelve

Harold hadn't blacked out completely. He had known when the men picked him up, not gently, and when they had half walked him back into the Whitman house. So he hadn't got away. Psyche or soma, he thought drowsily. Probably I really wanted the attention. (The phrase was a bit of an inside joke, back in the hospital.)

He was drooping forward in a soft chair, his head hanging, his eyes half-closed. He should be *paying* attention, listening to their voices, watching their faces. Wasn't that what he had come for, to get for himself what sense he could of the truth about these people? Break some false old images? The trouble was, he had found out enough already. (Oh, Wendy . . .) So you broke an image that's been bugging you. And it bugs you plenty—although differently.

The room was quiet now. There had been a lot of loud talk and confusion in here until the big man, Myra's brother, had roared for order. Now, there was order. Myra's brother was talking on the telephone, giving instructions, asking for people to do things. "And I want a patrol car at the Whitman gates, and fast. I've got a couple of Conrad's men on them, now. No newsmen in here. No exceptions. *I'll* give out a story, when I'm ready. And lay on that ambulance. This kook is supposed to be feverish and I'm taking no chances."

Harold remembered that Myra was dead. And the whole thing over to her brother? Tough for him, Harold thought, and noticed that he wasn't afraid for himself. Funny. He'd been afraid. He'd been furious, too. Now, he felt neither. Myra was dead, and that was a terrible thing and there would have to be consequences. He was in the path of the consequences. They were going to happen to *him,* and he understood that.

But Harold wasn't feeling much. Just . . . like a little tugging, like a whole lot of little arrows being drawn out of his very skin, all pointing across the room, over there, where Wendy was sitting close to that Mungo fellow, sitting quietly, as if she, too, were in a trance, much like his. (Oh, Wendy . . .)

He heard Edie speak up. "Please, Mr. Tyler, if you would only . . ."

She was sitting on the ottoman at his knees, bright-eyed, watching intently for a chance to fight for him. She was on Harold's side; he guessed he knew most of her reasons. Some sad, he thought. This was a sad house, altogether.

Tyler's deep voice spoke behind his head. "Just be quiet."

Ted Whitman said, "Charles, *I* think you ought to—"

Tyler barked, "I'm in charge, here."

Oh, he was. He had made them all sit down and be quiet. If Harold turned his head a bit he would be able to see Granny, in a chair the other side of the fireplace. He had looked at her once, but she wouldn't meet his eyes. She never had, he mused. Harold couldn't remember either of his own grandmothers. He had tried,

160

in the days of his marriage, to be very polite and respectful to old Mrs. Whitman, but he had never quite been able to follow what she was saying. The old lady had always confused him and made him feel uncomfortable. Wendy had no respect. Wendy used to laugh and brush her off.

(Oh, Wendy . . .)

Then there was Mr. Whitman, who always seemed to be very very busy and never getting anything actually done. Wendy had either wheedled something out of him or brushed him off, too. Harold had a freakish flash of concern for Mr. Whitman. Myra would have kept his fortune for him. His mother couldn't live forever. But Myra . . . being dead . . . Funny, he used to be afraid of them all.

Edie said to Mr. Tyler, "If you arrest Harold Page, I don't think you realize the damage you'll be doing."

But Charles Tyler knew exactly what he was doing. He had come here, in Ted Whitman's car, part the kindly brother-in-law and joint mourner. He now awaited the arrival of assistance, because he was the Chief of Police with a job to do. There was a little more to the apprehension of a criminal than the physical matter of putting him in one place rather than another. Tyler knew evidence when he saw it, testimony when he heard it. It was up to him to "get" the murderer and that was exactly what he was going to do. This little twerp from out of town, this social worker, wasn't going to tell him how to do it.

He said, "Harold Page is under arrest, right now."

"But I told you. He wasn't here on Wednesday."

Tyler hadn't told *her* anything yet, but he remembered all she had told him. Crazy. Not that crazy things didn't happen. On the contrary, they often did. It was a crazy thing, for instance, that his sister was dead, the

161

way she was.

But he had what it took, right now, to arrest the kook at least for attacking Myra on Wednesday night. "Seen running from the scene." He'd get what it took to put him on the scene of the actual murder. And it wouldn't be "crazy."

Tyler moved to where he could look down on the kook. Clean enough looking kid, which didn't mean a thing. Noticed with anger what he was wearing. Noticed what he was not wearing. Noticed the gray socks.

"You tell me he walked seventy-five miles?" said Tyler blandly. Disbelief was deep enough to sound polite.

"Ridiculous!" piped Ted.

"Nobody would do such a thing," pronounced old Mrs. Whitman, "not even a madman!"

They were gnats in Tyler's ears. He paid no heed.

It wasn't too wise for him to touch this kid, but he wanted to see the eyes. He put his palm on the boy's forehead and shoved the head back. The eyes were a little sad and cloudy.

"That's right? You *walked* seventy-five miles, did you?" Tyler was loud, as to a foreigner.

The boy's eyes brightened and widened as if with an impulse to smile and then saddened. He said, "Yes, sir."

He didn't try to explain. He can't explain, thought Tyler, who didn't want an explanation, anyhow. It would only be kookie. The question was, *Had* he walked? He limped. The Chief had seen that.

"You can prove you walked? You can prove you were someplace else on Wednesday night? Eh?"

The boy blinked. He seemed to search his memory. "I don't think so," he said. "There was only this dog . . ."

162

"Dog!" Tyler exploded.

"He slept on a lawn swing," Edie was saying rapidly. "A vacant house. Somebody may have seen him."

Tyler shut her up with one look. He supposed he'd have to waste somebody's time, someday, to go wherever this lawn swing was supposed to be, see if there *was* a lawn swing. Interview a dog? Augh. . . .

He looked down at the boy, who bore his gaze, not seeming to be too nervous. Kooks often were not, especially when they ought to be.

Tyler could hear the Whitman girl murmuring, across the room, "Can't we go now? To Mexico?"

And Ronnie Mungo's quick, "No, no."

Go to Mexico? thought Tyler with an inner snort. That was a Whitman for you. This kid, Wendy, was a witness; she couldn't go. As for Mungo — well, Mungo was no kook. Tyler had some questions for Mungo. There were things Tyler knew about Mungo, and there were some things he was going to want to know. He would find out, all right. But not now.

Now, think about the evidence against Harold Page. Also, about the testimony in his favor. Here was this girl social worker. Was she some kind of kook, too? "You say you've had him hidden, in this house, since yesterday afternoon at about two o'clock?"

"Yes, sir." She didn't explain, either.

The Whitman twitter began. Ted said, "Impossible!" The old lady said, "Preposterous!"

But, although unlikely, it was not impossible. Tyler had heard of cases. He himself had known one attic case, where a woman had hidden a deformed child from her second husband, in the same house, some eleven years. The Whitmans might not have known that Harold Page was in their house for one night.

They didn't know much, in his opinion.

163

The old lady was a relic. Oh, she was smart, in her way. She kept her status. It had not diminished. People tended to kowtow. She had both social and economic power in the town. She watched over the Whitman money, or watched her hired hands watch it. But she didn't know anything about the world at the bottom of the hill, and never had, he reflected. As for Ted, there was a joke in the town. The Estate managers were said to pay one man a handsome salary to do one thing only — keep Ted Whitman's fingers out of any and all pies. Ted was an idiot.

And Myra had to marry *him!* Well, Myra had been, her brother supposed, ready to settle for this. Myra had run around . . . and in circles . . . for quite some time. She'd had it, on romance, Tyler supposed. If that was what it could be called.

She was dead, now. Murdered. *His* case.

He focused on this Edith Thompson. He'd like to be rid of her nuisance quality right now. "You tell me why," he snapped. "Why would you hide this man in your room? You in love with him?" A somewhat kookie reason, but existent.

Her face was pale and she started to get to her feet. "It was because I didn't believe—"

"Sit down," he snapped and it was as if he had shoved her.

She didn't *believe!* Oh, deliver me from kooks. And fools. And bleeding hearts.

Wendy Whitman popped up from her spot on the sofa, like a jack-in-the-box with its spring released. "She let him in! She hid him! He could have killed somebody!" the girl wailed.

Tyler glanced at the boy and the boy's face was as bare as bone, and pure pain.

Ted was trotting after his daughter, who circled the

floor behind the sofa like a distressed animal. "Criminal! Absolutely criminal! Now, sweetheart . . ."

The old lady was leaning forward. "You, guard!" She spoke to Conrad, who stood back of Harold's chair. "You are paid to keep your eye on him. On the madman, remember!"

The guard said, "Yes, ma'am."

And Charles Tyler felt like sweeping the whole pack of Whitmans out of his way with one brush of his arm.

Deliver me, not only from kooks and fools, but spoiled brats, useless idiots, and rich old women.

The guard, Conrad, spoke up. "Excuse me, Chief Tyler, but I guess you remember? — I was in here, going through every room, yesterday afternoon? Before we put the guards on?"

And Tyler turned to him with some relief. This was his language.

"You weren't in *my* room," spoke up Edie Thompson, speaking the language, too, and with spirit.

Edie was feeling better, now that Harold Page was in the open. It was not her nature to hide in corners. She was more or less the happy warrior, now — fighting openly, although she could think of nothing else to do but dispute every word that was, to her *knowledge,* not true. Her truth wasn't going to sound true. Her reasons hadn't sounded very reasonable. Nobody wanted to believe that she had done what she had done, and she couldn't blame them.

The guard gave her a nod that agreed, and went on: "I was going to say, I searched that room, up there (That's your room, miss?) around midnight, and he wasn't in it then. She knows and Mr. Whitman, he can tell you, too. We . . ."

165

Edie opened her mouth to answer the look on Charles Tyler's face, to "explain" the truth about where Harold Page had been, around midnight, but before she could phrase a sentence that would have the slightest chance of sounding true or reasonable at all, Cousin Ted cut in.

"Of course he wasn't there. Now, this is what really happened, Charles." He was up and balanced on his tiny feet, his face flushed with victorious understanding. Cousin Ted had it all figured out.

Tyler listened in moody silence; he was more or less just waiting. But things could come out.

"He got in here," said Cousin Ted, "on Wednesday night, by way of the tree. We know that. After he fought with my poor Myra, he ran away. We know that, because Wendy saw him. Very well." Ted was in ecstasy of logic. "Now, the house was searched on Thursday, yesterday, and he was *not* here. So it is obvious that Edie for some reasons of her own (which I, for one, simply cannot imagine) is only trying to give him an alibi. But the *point"* — Ted let out what was almost a crow — "the point is, Charles — the madman was not getting out just now. He was getting *in. Again!* That, alone, is against the law. Arrest him!"

Cousin Ted was really a ridiculous man. There he stood with his arm thrown out dramatically, in his own eyes the hero who had solved everything.

Tyler said, wearily, "I *have* arrested him. Waiting on the ambulance."

But Harold's eyes were slowly widening. So was Edie's mouth. "Wait a minute. What did he *say?*" There was a thing that Cousin Ted had said, that played back with a surprise in it.

Tyler seemed to suffer a playback of an idea.

He strode to Harold, took hold of the white coat,

gathering it close to Harold's throat. "This coat you're wearing," said Tyler. "That's how you could sneak into the hospital last night? Where my sister was lying in a coma, helpless, and you put the thing over her head? Where did you get this coat?"

Harold said, "My own."

"Absurd! Absurd!" Cousin Ted was almost dancing, behind them.

"Neck — look — neck — " choked Harold.

Tyler let go and seemed to fling the boy backward. Mistake to touch. He knew that. Better not. He said, bitterly, "I suppose there's no getting any sense out of him."

But Edie was up and in battle array. She cried out sharply to the big angry man, "Why don't you *look* inside his neckband?"

"What's that?"

"How do *you* know he doesn't make sense?" she howled.

His anger and hers met head-on. With a dark look on his face, Tyler turned again, and yanked Harold's torso forward, then the white coat backward. He read from the inside of the neckband — HAROLD PAGE. He tossed the boy against the chair.

"Nobody told *me* she was killed in the hospital," cried Edie.

("In the hospital!" someone echoed. Ronnie?)

"If that's so," Edie went on triumphantly, "then he happens to have an alibi. And what are you going to do about that?"

"Happens to wear a white coat?" Tyler said.

"Happens to have worked as an orderly in a hospital. Which happens to use white coats, *too*. What a coincidence!" She threw this in his teeth.

The clash was strange, this time, because it melted

167

into a kind of joining. He and she were, at least, clashing in the same terms.

Charles Tyler believed in coincidences, all right. He was the one who knew all about them. He kept a little working scale in his mind. One coincidence? Par for the course. A mere maybe. Two coincidences? Suspect. Watch it. Three coincidences? *No*. Almost always, significantly connected. A real freak, if not. So, putting the white coat on this scale, it was a mild "maybe."

"Maybe," he said sourly. He thought, But he's in town, and there's the second one.

Then Wendy Whitman, who had been shifting, moving, not quite pacing but flitting, as it were, back and forth, burst in. "I don't know what you people are talking about! Didn't you hear her *say* she let him in? And hid him! *She* didn't care if he murdered us or not. She doesn't even *belong* in this house."

"Thank God!" flashed Edie.

And Tyler was startled by the antagonism between the two of them, the blond girl and the dark one, the poor girl and the rich one (whichever was which). It burned like a naked flame. Tyler's mind said, Ah! What's all this? His mind was also tucking away something about this social worker. In his experience, *they* were not fire-spitting types. They were trained out of it. They were trained, he often thought, out of every emotion known to man but one—which they called "compassion" and which consisted of having no human feelings of their very ego-own.

Maybe he had this social worker wrong. She *was* a young one. He looked at the kook, this Harold Page. These females wouldn't be fighting over *him*, surely. What the devil was that skinned look on the kook's face?

Harold could feel his ears grow, so hard was he listening. Wendy was behind his field of vision, somewhere in this big room. *He* couldn't see her. He heard the antagonism, yes. But more. He could hear the fear. But Wendy was not afraid of him, as he alone could know. What was she afraid of, then? Phantoms, maybe? Or punishment? He wished he could know. He wished he could look at her and talk to her. He felt so funny—as if his thumbs were pricking.

Scared? thought Tyler. What scared him, just now?

He sent a piercing gaze to Edie. "What is your relationship with this man, Edith?" he said coldly. "Why are you so bound and determined to get him out of this?"

"Because he doesn't belong in it. He is *not* that nice convenient figure, the 'berserk ex-husband.' "

Insult me, thought Tyler. Good. Get worked up, and tell me something. "You intended," he went on, "to smuggle him out and never mention a wanted man to the authorities?"

"*You* were the authority, yesterday," she said. "That's why I stopped and thought better of mentioning it." Then, her face broke and she smiled at him. "I made a mistake, I think."

Tyler said nothing. Flattery would get her nowhere.

At least, thought Edie, she had his attention and that was good. She was standing up, now, and he hadn't told her to sit down. She went on as vehemently as she could. "But I'll tell you and swear to this. Harold Page certainly did not get into Myra's hospital room last night because he was here, with guards all around, and I myself was with him, nearly all night long."

169

Granny said, "All night long! Disgraceful!"

Edie flashed around to look at her. "Then *you* believe me, Granny?"

"I do not," said Granny, loftily, "*care* to believe you, Edith."

Edith chewed on her lip and faced Tyler. Did something stir behind his cold gray look? "My word should be as good as *that,* at least," she said.

"Back it up," he said coldly.

"Well, Dr. Wesley knows." Edie thought, How strange to have to *prove* it!

"Who is he and how does he know what?"

"He is Harold's doctor." She saw the flaw. "Well, I *told* him on the telephone—but earlier this morning. And Ronnie Mungo knows."

Ronnie Mungo, long ago, had retreated to the outer fringes where he remained an interested spectator. As soon as the draperies had opened, in fact, Ronnie had abandoned the cause as if he had never joined it. He had been sitting beside Wendy, when Wendy had been sitting, but merely beside her. Now he sat alone on the sofa, with his pleasant smile, his air of having better manners than to interfere in any way, masking him completely.

Tyler challenged, "You go along with that? Mungo? You knew Harold Page was hidden in this house?"

"Let me put it this way," said Ron, with an easy air, yet as if he wished to be scrupulously truthful. "I *believed* that he was here, when the lady said so." He was neatly and pleasantly being on both sides at once. Then he added, "I believe it now, don't you?"

Before Tyler could speak, Wendy, hanging over the back of the sofa, with her hair down over her face, said as if she were cursing, "He *was* here. He *was* here. How long are you going to *talk* about it? How long are you going to *talk?*" She seemed to be cracking with something.

Scared? Tyler wondered.

Down in the round cellar at the base of the tower, it was almost dark. The tiny slits of windows, at ground level, were filthy and shrubs grew close. It was chilly, down there within the circling stone. Sound did not penetrate that stone or down so deep. Nor could a small whimper, near the floor, escape as far as an ear, upstairs.

In the big room, Ronnie Mungo hushed Wendy, with a touch of annoyance. "Be a little quiet, toots."

"Can't we get out?" She sounded as if she must get out or die.

"No, no. Not now."

"Never?" said Wendy, like a child who had learned a new word recently, but did not like the taste of it. She pushed herself away from the sofa and went to the stairs, where she dragged up two steps. She sat down on the fourth step and put both her hands on the iron balusters. She peered through, between two of them, as if she were in a prison cell, looking out.

Tyler watched her, thinking, Well, *this* one's a kook, for sure. He knew Wendy by reputation. He had daughters. Wendy was willful and wild, unsatisfactory as a friend. None of the young people who swam in the currents, down in the town, busy with their lives, could be bothered to put up with her.

What a bunch! he thought, looking around the room. The old lady was glaring at her granddaughter with a curled lip. Ted had frozen between flutters.

There was neither repose nor purpose in him. And Myra took this every day? what a crew!

He turned his mind sternly to Ronnie Mungo. Sticking in Tyler's craw was the query: Why in hell did *Mungo* go for that rescue bit with this Edith-social-worker-person?

Oh, he would find out, once he got his witnesses where he could go to work on them, one by one, with all the skill and patience that he possessed. Where the devil was that ambulance and the others?

Tyler told Conrad to watch it and went up into the foyer and outside. Air was good. He breathed deep and tried to track the notion about Mungo that was stirring somewhere in his head. What if Mungo would rather the Page kid didn't have an alibi? Pretty vague. Pretty fancy. But something like that.

Chapter Thirteen

A police car raced up the drive and pulled up at his very feet, with a flourish. Ah! Another one, down at the gates. Ah, more like it!

"Where's the ambulance?" he demanded.

"Dunno, sir."

"Check on it. Must be some foul-up."

"You got the kook in there, Chief? We'll take him in."

"Nope," said Tyler. "Trouble enough, without 'police brutality.' "

His men grinned, showing appreciation.

"Roust up that ambulance and you . . . sit here. Just sit on it."

"Yes, sir."

"It's a snake pit," he told them. "One of those."

They were using the com. Tyler stepped back toward the house. Stood, gazing over the town. His town.

He had a snake pit up here, all right. One of those damn cases with plenty of meat for columnists and commentators. He foresaw the chewing-over, the speculation, the theories and the counter-theories, spun out, like Ted Whitman's, on shaky premises. The shakier the more fun. All the "logical" trappings of the whodunit, a gamboling of brains. And the hearts bleeding for Harold Page. They always bled for the accused. Not for Myra, who was dead. No fun in that. The accused might turn out innocent. Myra would not turn up alive.

He had to apprehend her murderer.

And what if the kook's alibi stood up? Guaranteed, by the very guards appointed to frustrate him? Then, somebody else was the murderer.

Tyler already had an alternate in mind, although it was, as yet, pure speculation. Mungo. Once upon a time, as Charles Tyler had known, Mungo and Myra had been pretty cozy. What if she had made some kind of threat, trying to stop Mungo from getting married to the kid with the money? Mungo was trapped, all right. Tyler had heard it on the grapevine. He'd gone through money like he had his own mint, and he had paid off two very expensive wives in his day. Never earned a nickel, either. A sporting type, this Mungo. Traveler, sailor, tennis player. Tyler thought that one could begin to feel a little less spry on a tennis court as one grew older.

Suppose rich boy is against the wall and here is little rich girl, spoiling to get her hands on her mama's money and Mungo wants, in the worst way, to help her do just that? In the worst way? Bad enough to kill?

Would Myra risk the threat, though, when to make it good she would expose herself, too, and what would Ted Whitman do then, poor schmoe? Tyler didn't know, but guessed, that Ted would put his head back in the sand as fast as he could. The old lady was a different proposition. She might boot out Mungo, and Myra, too. Myra would have been taking a risk. Had she been torchy enough for Mungo, still? Jealous? Women had their motives and Tyler was the first to admit that he didn't always understand them. He knew some that seemed to exist. He had a glimpse, now, and his mind said, Ah! Myra wouldn't be crazy about finding herself Ronnie Mungo's *stepmother.* It rang authentically female.

But in spite of the ring of this, he was really reaching and he knew it. Wishful, even? Maybe so. He resented this Mungo, but he knew that he did. So Tyler's mind came heavily over to the other side. Not likely *Mungo,* prowling the hospital, when eight out of ten pairs of female eyes would have noticed him. Why was that? Tyler didn't know. But he knew it was so.

Well, he thought, get back in and maybe stir up a little more and keep listening. He'd get down statements later on. But before a story crystallizes, you can often catch on to a whole lot of loose ends, handy for pulling when you need them. The crystallizing process, as he well knew, was a smoothing-out process. What didn't fit got cast aside. Truth got tailored. Maybe he could get hold of a little more of the raw stuff.

The cop came to tell him that the ambulance had gone to the *hospital!* And, oh, the cop knew that Tyler wasn't going to see anything funny *about* it, and the whole department, in fact, quivered in anticipation of his blast. For such a foul-up!

But Tyler, with his cold look, said, "Get on to the ambulance. Tell them, no noise. And when they get here, if they ever do, hold them. Just let me know."

He turned to go in—a man who recognized pressure when he had it, and who now thought he might as well use what pressure had come into his hand.

Let them squirm.

* * *

The big room was silent, now that Granny was off the phone. The moment Tyler had left them, she'd been on it, ordering her doctor to her side, immediately, and if he was with another patient, then let another doctor tend to that patient. She was Lila Whitman. Now she was at the far end of the sofa, in another chair, and Ronnie Mungo was hovering in attendance.

Edith was trying to seize on silence to organize herself and think how to be more effective. But the silence was a distraction. She wished Wendy wouldn't sit on the stairs and stare, like an animal in a cage. Granny hadn't gone near her. Her own father hadn't gone near her. Where the dickens is Mrs. Beck, all this time? she thought.

Harold could barely sense where Wendy was — his mate, his love, his hate, his enemy — and he none of these to her. There was nothing he could do anymore, with her, to her, for her, or against her. All lines between them had been cut long ago. He put his heavy head back, to wait on fate. When had they been divorced? he wondered. What and who had put them asunder when they were young? Something had worked on Wendy while he'd had to be away. He could swear to that, now. Where was Mrs. Beck, by the way?

Charles Tyler stood at the top of the two steps and thought, Well, there they are. The whole crew! Or was there someone missing?

Granny, at sight of him, began severely. "This is making me very very nervous, Charles. I have called Dr. Brewster and I shall take his advice when he comes. I cannot see why I should be required to endure this sort of thing, or why you do not simply remove him. That mad person."

Ted, as if she'd touched one of his buttons, began to chime, "You had better take him away, Charles. That murdering monster! Or I don't promise . . ." Which was ridiculous. Ted, playing that he was on the verge of vengeful violence, when he couldn't, at the moment, seem to struggle out of his chair.

Tyler said, "Sit still. Be a couple of minutes." He came to stand behind the "murdering monster," making a muttered request to Conrad, who at once went briskly to the foyer where he would know exactly when the ambulance came.

The boy was sitting quietly, his fine hands relaxed. Young hands, corrected Tyler. Most young hands look fine.

Edie said to Tyler quietly, "He had no reason on earth to do anything to Myra."

(She was thinking, And you know he didn't do it.)

But now Ted bounced up. "She is talking about motive, Charles," he explained. (And Edie saw humor flash in Tyler's eyes.) "That's very simple." Ted puffed up. "He killed her so that Myra wouldn't tell."

"Tell what?" said Edie flatly.

"Why, that he had attacked her!"

"Why had he attacked her?"

"Because. He want to kill her, of course." Cousin Ted left his mouth open and panted softly. "What?"

Edie couldn't help it. She laughed. She looked up at Tyler and said, "Excuse me. I'm sorry. But if *that* doesn't go round and round . . ."

The Chief of Police said, broodingly, "No. It often happens pretty much that way. People trying to cover up bad with worse. They fool themselves that this will fix it."

Edie knew that her whole face reacted to accept his correction and to agree with him. Hadn't she listened, time and again, to people of all ages telling long sequences of "good" reasons for doing wrong? Being sucked on downward, spiraling down and down, and ever explaining that they swam with purpose, ever intending to come to a turning place, when all of the past wrongs would be covered up, at last, and they could rise up again.

"Looking for the turning-around place," she said aloud.

Then her heart gave a bit of a happy jump because the big policeman knew what she meant, respected her phrase, and accepted her as one who also knew these things. We are getting on, she thought, if we are beginning to communicate. She had begun to think of his eyes as intelligent, not cold.

But now Wendy was blown off the stairs as if she had been picked up by the wind. She was down on the carpet, whirling like a leaf in a storm. It was as if her long cramped immobility had exploded with an accumulation of the need to move. It seemed she would dance away into the dining room. But she did not go. She whirled back and wound up slap against the back of the sofa, where she clung.

Tyler eyed her warily. Harold shut his eyes tight. Granny said tartly, "Now, Wendy . . . Now, I was *afraid* . . . This is *just* the sort of thing, Charles . . . It's too much for a sensitive child. Not to mention *me*. Where *is* Mrs. Beck?" Granny was on her feet. "We pay the woman. Take him away, Charles. Do. You know as well as I do that Harold Page needs no motive."

"Oh, *he* doesn't need a thing," said Edie, with hot eyes. "Not even the opportunity."

178

She looked to Tyler to resume communication, but she seemed to have lost him. "The prison ward is the place for him," said Tyler. He seemed to be watching Ronnie Mungo, who had scrambled up and was now beside Wendy with an arm around her. Wendy was suddenly as still as stone again.

Edie thought, This policeman has to understand, and he will. I believe he will. She rose and went closer to Tyler. "No, it isn't the place for him, sir. Especially not for him. I wish you'd let me tell you . . ."

"We don't abuse a prisoner," Tyler said.

"I don't mean that. I am thinking of his child."

"You are fond of the child, are you?" His eyes pierced.

"I've never seen the child."

"What is your motive, then?" Tyler sounded patient. "I wouldn't mind understanding your motive."

"But they are making him the scapegoat. They did that once before. He came because he cares for the child. Surely, the child has to be thought of. I am concerned, because, don't you see, that if you . . ."

Wendy called out, like her old self, rude, ruthless, "Listen to her! Carrying on about the child. The child! What a hypocrite! What did she care, when she hid the madman in our house? *She* decided he wasn't dangerous. Well, *we* thought he was dangerous and it's *our* house. What kind of big old concern is that?"

Oh, Wendy was slippery. Wendy could make sense. The antagonism was raw — but there was reason in what she said.

"Certainly," said Cousin Ted.

Chapter Fourteen

Mrs. Beck was pretty sure that her upper right arm was broken or perhaps her shoulder, by the feel of it. Her face felt bashed in on one side and she didn't want to touch it with her one usable hand. Her legs, however, seemed to work and on them she had crawled slowly up the steep and narrow stone stairs, not thinking of anything but the pain and how to get relief from the pain. Now, she sat in a heap on the tiny landing, not much more than a top step, just inside the door. The door was ajar, just slightly. She could smell the smells of the house, the upper living house and she could hear living voices. Knock? she was thinking. Thrust? Be enough to sag upon the door. It would open. She would be in the light. But—wait. Might as well be careful.

Harold had found a little vigor for his voice. "Wendy is right, Edie. Let it go, now. Don't you be in any more trouble."

Tyler snapped, "This a confession?"

"No, sir," said Harold, "but there will be due process. I can afford a lawyer, this time."

"Due process!" said Granny. "The impudence!

Well, we shall have *our* lawyers." She started to walk, as if to the phone again.

Wendy bent over as if her spine snapped and was draped over the sofa-back, her hair hanging to brush the cushions. Ron reached to try to lift her upright and Granny said, with a fastidious flutter of her dainty nostrils, "Do put that child down somewhere, Mr. Mungo, and keep her calm. Wendy, my advice is simply that you must rise above this whole sickening vulgar business until the doctor comes."

And Mrs. Beck, biting on pain, thought, Wait a minute. Wendy was there, was she? And *how* was she? This was very important. Mrs. Beck knew very well that she and Wendy—never mind a broken bone or two—might still be in the same boat. And did they have the madman?

Granny said, "Ingratitude! We took Edith in, Charles, when my niece died. For two years in this house, she had everything she could possibly want. She chose to leave."

And Ted began to echo and embellish. "Ungrateful! Resentful, too! Always did resent our Wendy. Envy, you know. Why, all this is nothing in the world but—"

"But *what?*" howled Edie. She had begun to shake. All right, admitted that she had been foolish. Led deeper and deeper, after a first step she ought never to have taken. It seemed months ago that she had thought to be, for an hour perhaps, the gentle go-between, wise for both sides. But just the same, she would take no more of the Whitman brand of nonsense. "Nothing in the world but what?" she shouted, being human and humanly enraged, because she had tried to be grateful for their "everything" and she had failed. "Spite?" cried Edie. "Do you think I am making up his alibi just to annoy you? Or do you think I

181

brought him into this house hoping that he *would* kill you all off?"

Tyler was looking at her. Nothing in his look condemned her for being human, but he was the judge, just the same. He was sane. And Edie felt ashamed. Even Cousin Ted could say a true thing. Edie did resent them. Resented Wendy. She had meant no harm, but she had taken risks. Tears swam into her eyes. "If I had let *him* run the risk of being shot on Thursday—at least there wouldn't have been a scapegoat." (And now she was shaking because that was true. And would Myra, then, have died?)

"A scapegoat for whom?" said Myra's brother.

Mrs. Beck licked her dusty lip. That Edith—carrying on. Well, Mrs. Beck could hold against the pain for another minute. She had better. She didn't know the smart thing to do. She didn't know, for instance, why they weren't looking for her. Something funny . . . Now she could hear the old woman, very close.

"Charles, if it were not for you, I would call the *police*. In fact, I think if you cannot control this situation you ought to resign."

She must be at the telephone. Mrs. Beck's thigh ached, where the stone edge of a step pressed into it. Her whole torso was aching. Her head whirled.

"As it is," Granny picked up the phone, "I *shall* call my lawyer." She was dialing the operator. "Edith, you know," she said haughtily to Tyler, "was brought up to believe that all poor people are saints and angels, but anyone with means must be a villain. That's why she's on his side. It's psychological." Granny was being gentle with the ignorant.

Edie put all of her fingers into her hair. "Poor people come in all kinds, Granny," she said, shakily.

"Certainly they do," snapped Mrs. Whitman, with her own superb illogic, "but *you* don't *know* that."

Then she was grandly commanding the operator to reach her lawyer for her. The operator began to be extremely tiresome, seeming to think she needed the number. Ronnie Mungo came to help.

Harold was thinking about wealth. At the moment, he had very little cash. About a dollar and a half, he thought. He'd had enough saved from his meager salary to pay a week's advance on the room in the boardinghouse. Enough left to get him down here, and back, on the bus. He hadn't saved any money by walking. It had cost him more, having to eat so many times. He wondered if money would have made any difference, in those days.

"The will isn't through probate yet," he said aloud. "I borrowed on it, though, for my tuition."

"What's that?" Tyler said, in a moment.

"My great-uncle's will. He was quite wealthy." Harold looked up, because there was a peculiar silence. Everything was stopped.

"You can check," said Harold.

To Edie, it was very funny. It was hysterical. "Everybody change sides," she sang out blithely. "I'll be against him, and all of you can be *for* him."

"That," said Tyler severely, "will do — from you."

"I should think so," said Granny grimly.

Ronnie Mungo, having gone to her aid, was on the phone for her. He rolled an eye across the room, turned his back, began to speak, conveying Granny's orders. Granny left him to do it and huffed her way back to the far chair. "Edith," she said, "I shall change my will. Don't *imagine* that I won't!"

Ronnie Mungo kicked at the cellar door and it

183

closed with a sharp click. Mrs. Beck made a little yelp. It was no louder than a mouse-squeak. Then, she sagged in darkness.

Cousin Ted was snatching at his chance to be forceful. "Edith," he said, "*I* suggest that you pack your things."

"Yes, indeed," said Granny, and Ted swelled with her approval. (He had said the right thing.)

"Very well," said Edie calmly, "but I can't leave town. Can I, Mr. Tyler?"

"No," he said. But his attention wasn't on her. He wasn't following the family clash. He had the feeling that something else was going on here, and he was missing it. His eyes slid to watch Mungo as he came slouching toward Granny, the courteous male, having done her telephoning for her. Oh, quite the little helper around here. But "not involved." You bet not, thought Tyler. So what has got him shaking in his boots, all of a sudden?

Edie was saying, "I'll have to stay to make a statement. I believe that Wendy fought with Myra, Wednesday night."

Granny burst furiously, "Now, she *cannot* say that, Charles. Shut her up, if you please? At once!"

(Not I, thought Tyler.)

"They fought, I think," said Edie, steadily, "over Wendy's engagement to Ronnie Mungo."

Mungo was leaning on the wall now, behind Granny. He looked as if he would like to crawl through it.

"Back that up, Edith," said Tyler sternly, even as his mind said Ah!

"Mrs. Beck could back that up for you," said Edie. "Where is she?"

That was when Wendy toppled over. Just as she was, where Ron had left her, huddled on the sofa, with her arms still tight around her knees, she fell sideways and lay in the knot. "I don't know where Becky is. I don't want to hear anymore. I wish you would get this over." She uncurled convulsively and lay on her face with her wrists against her ears and her fingers clawed, stiffly. "I want Becky," she whimpered.

Mrs. Beck, lying on her side on the tiny platform, legs trailing down, her neck bent where her head was against the lowest board of the cellar door, could hear very clearly. For some reason, sound came through the low slot, the natural crack at the bottom of the door, and was reflected directly into her ear.

Now, though her head swam, her nostrils flared, scenting hope, scenting power. But she couldn't move, not yet. Couldn't reach up and turn the doorknob. Couldn't twist and raise until her good hand and arm could do that. In physical weakness, she must wait. And listen. Carefully.

Tyler said to Edie, "Do you accuse Wendy of getting into the hospital last night? Of putting a pliofilm bag over my sister's head until she died? Of watching her die? Of waiting—to take the bag off, afterwards?"

His words were brutal and Edie winced away from them. Like *that?* No passionate half-accident? (Oh, did the damaged brain know what was happening? Did the body struggle? The blind unconscious organism's will to live?) She gasped. "No, I don't, sir. I didn't know . . . it was . . . like that. I don't know."

"Or," said Tyler, "do you think it was Mungo did *that?*"

Chapter Fifteen

Mungo kept his hands in his pockets but swayed forward from the support of the wall. "If that's what is on your mind," he said, "check it. I took Wendy to a party with twenty people there. At Sandy Waltham's. We left when they can tell you and arrived here when the guard, over there, can say. You check it. Find out there wasn't time." He sounded bold and angry.

"And after you left here?" said Tyler, without apparent emotion.

"I went directly to the Broken Drum, where I am known. Got a little drunk and a fellow went home with me. We kicked life around until the sun was up. Ask him. Paul Milliman."

"I'll do that," said Tyler.

"And I got here this morning," Mungo went on, "when, Edith can tell you. And the guard, too."

Tyler said, "Thank you very much." And saw Mungo flush a little. He sure overdid *that*, Tyler thought.

Well—the Chief thought he'd gotten about as much as he would get, here. He'd start the check on Mungo. Might be late. The criminal has the advantage of knowing what to cover up before the police can know it. This Mungo was no kook. The Chief realized that it would be a pleasure to "get" him.

He glanced at Conrad, who nodded. So the ambulance was out there. Tyler said, "Okay. We'll take Page now."

He had forgotten about Edie for a moment.

Edie said, "You are taking Wendy, too, of course."

And Tyler sighed invisibly.

"She has been accused. As much as he has. Or wasn't it against the law for *her* to knock Myra down? Is Wendy immune?"

Might as well be, the Chief thought. Don't fight it, little social worker. I can't take her on your belief. You weren't here.

"Well, I can tell you," said Edie, hotly, "that she has always been a liar, that she faked a beating, and said Harold did it, to get her divorce. In fact, she's not exactly normal. She doesn't give one damn about her own baby. Or much else. She's unstable enough to have hallucinations, just about. And rages! Don't you believe me? Shall I *put* her into a tantrum? Right here and now? It's not very difficult."

The Whitmans were stricken dumb.

Harold Page was the one who stopped her with his sudden cry. "Ah, don't! Don't, Edie. Please? Don't hit her. You've hated her long enough."

He was so impelled that he started to get up, to go to Wendy, but the guard leaped and put a quick strong arm in his way.

Tyler watched Edie go up to the big window and stand there with her back to the room. He thought, Honey, you are probably right, which is nothing to be ashamed of, in my book. But who *killed* Myra? You don't know.

Granny had found breath and said, "I would advise *nobody* to listen to that insanely ungrateful girl. And until this trash is out of my house, *I* shall not listen at all." She then, with a flourish, turned off her hearing aid.

Tyler said glumly, "I'm in charge here." And then to Conrad, "Just hold everything." And he went into the foyer to open the front door and call his people himself. He'd get one of them to pass along instructions for the checking up on Ronnie Mungo. He was thinking sadly, How weak is reason, against the very root of force. He couldn't condemn Edith Thompson for a touch of human passion.

In the big room, Conrad hung over Harold.

Harold knew he couldn't get to her, but might he dare speak? The old lady was very stiff and blank of face. Couldn't hear. Ted Whitman, in a comical way, looked deaf, too. Mungo was leaning on the wall, kind of out of it. Edie was by the window. The big Chief was gone.

"Ah, Wendy . . ." He said it. The crying of his heart was in the timbre of his voice. "I wish you could have talked to me, whatever it is. I wish I could have listened, in those days. But I thought . . . I was young. I thought you had everything."

No one stirred.

"What was it that you wanted?" he asked, in another moment.

No answer.

"Why did you ever marry me?" If he could only reach her, this one last chance.

She rolled her dark head, suddenly. "I forget," said Wendy drearily.

"Now you want to marry him? So much?" "Hell-

188

bent," Edie had said. Harold was breaking his heart to understand.

"I don't know," said Wendy faintly.

"I wish I could have figured out what it was you really wanted. I wish you could have come away with me, and lived in an apartment." He did wish that. He did wish she could have got away from here.

"That was not for me," she said. "Not for me."

But why not for her? he wondered. "Did you feel . . . so bad," he asked her, "about the baby's ears?"

"No," said Wendy. "Not for me, that's all. Not for me." It was so dreary. She sounded as if she had always been defeated.

"Wendy, do you love . . . ?" He was thinking about sermons that said you must love or perish. He didn't know how to finish.

"I don't know what you mean," she said, wiggling. "Don't *talk*." Then she raised up. *"Anywhere,"* she burst. "I wish . . ." But she didn't say what she wished so fervently.

Harold said, gently, "If I could do it all over again, I would. I wish I could." He wasn't asking for the future. He waited to know whether she understood his basic apology for not having been what she wanted. "Do you know that?"

In a moment, Wendy's head fell and turned slowly to bury one ear. Her hand came up and covered the other. Harold guessed it didn't matter whether she knew. She didn't care. It was an answer of sorts. "I'm truly sorry," he murmured. The strong arm, that had been something to lean against, now seemed to be helping him sink back. He wanted to say thanks but he didn't, couldn't. Love and let go.

Edie stared out the window. She had hated Wendy. She had let her temper go, just now, and that wasn't

189

any good either. Anger and hate. The destroyers. She heard, in Harold's voice, what was right. To try to understand, to forgive, to go on loving. (Oh, poor kid!) Well, that's fine, she thought. That's right and good, I guess. BUT. ALSO. MEANWHILE. She rebelled, fiercely.

She looked up into the tree and thought that there was a huge and flaming BUT, and a hard ALSO, and an urgent MEANWHILE. It was a good and useful idea to learn to dissipate the destructive emotions that ate on one's own insides. The boy had learned to do it, in order to save himself.

BUT, was it enough, just to save yourself from that? When long before you could "save" somebody like Wendy, you had to fight what she *did?* Didn't you? MEANWHILE, she mustn't be allowed to go on, ruthlessly lying and destroying. Oh yes, try to understand her. ALSO try to stop her. If you could stop her, without hating her, so·much the better. But she had to be stopped, just the same. My father was wrong, in part, she thought. Or I'm not like him. No, I am not like him. I thought I was. She turned.

Tyler was coming in. The ambulance men were behind him—two in white coats—to take Harold away. Harold agreed. He was even now trying to get to his feet. Poor kid! Chewed up in this house, and spat out, and never mind his pain? His injuries?

Edie thought, But here is a wrong. And it is Wendy's doing, this wrong. It's her false witness that is forcing them to take him as a suspect. Why doesn't my witness count? Can't I stop it?

It seemed she hadn't. So it was dead-end, frustration alley. The police would take the scapegoat off to a prison ward, for another black mark on him and another martyrdom. Harold would survive. But would he ever get his child?

Edie had been in on custody cases. She could hear a judge saying, "In view of the fact that he is a young man, alone—in view, also, of his psychiatric history *and* his police record."

"Your Honor, he was acquitted."

"I am aware of that. Even so, in view of the circumstances and position of the mother's family, and this child's affliction—all things taken together—for the best good of the child . . ."

But the Whitmans would *not* be for the best good of the child.

So, you kicked and screamed a little, but then your wits began to work like rats, hunting and searching for some way to *stop* them.

Granny said, suddenly and imperiously, from her frozen face that looked blind because she could not hear. "Will someone be kind enough to bring me a glass of cold water?"

And Edie was up on her toes.

"Mr. Tyler." Her tone turned him. "There is a glass on the mantelpiece. When he came, yesterday, he was very hot and tired. That glass has my fingerprints and Harold's on it. When did we put them there? Have you seen him offered anything? Don't you think you ought to take along the evidence that proves his alibi?"

A kind of fading took place on Tyler's face. He followed her gesture and found the drinking glass. He teased it out of concealment, gingerly. The boys from the ambulance, and one of the cops from the car, were on the foyer steps. "Hold it a minute," Tyler said to them. (He hadn't for some time, seemingly, doubted that the Page kid had this nutty alibi.)

"All right," he said to Conrad savagely. "Now, you

191

run me down, right now, exactly who was in and out of here last night."

"I was on," Conrad said eagerly, "from midnight."

"Charles!" Ted yelped. "Surely . . ." You are my brother-in-law, the sentence finished, unsaid.

"Sit down," roared Tyler and blasted Ted back into the chair.

He looked around. Ted settled. The old lady sitting still, deaf as a post. *She* hadn't done it. Mungo, against the wall, keeping out of it in eighteen languages. Scared green, too. The Whitman kid, lying on her face. A nut. A kook. Harold Page half-up, sagged to rest on the arm of the chair. Edie Thompson standing there. "Sit down, Edith," Tyler said, in a normal voice that was not unkind.

She said, "Thank you."

"When I take over at midnight," Conrad was eager to show his mettle, "Carlson tells me that the old lady is in, and her . . ." Conrad flipped a finger toward Edie, "and Mr. Whitman, he'd come in, the middle of the evening. Now, the young lady on the couch, there—she and the boyfriend—they came in just about then. I saw myself that he didn't stay but a couple of minutes."

Granny said, in the loud voice of the totally deaf, breaking in without regard to anyone's thoughts but her own, "Are all of you deaf? I believe that I requested a glass of water."

Ronnie Mungo said smoothly, "May I fetch Mrs. Whitman her drink, sir?"

"Go ahead," said Tyler. (And if you run, boy, then I've got you.)

Mungo went edging along to the dining room door. Something was on his mind, all right. "And pretty soon," the guard was continuing, "comes the last one in, the housekeeper or whatever she is. And that's it, sir. And *nobody* got out."

"Where is Mrs. Beck, now?" said Tyler, in a tone that was unusually light for him.

He had better find out!

He sent the cop into the east wing. (The other cop was out in the car, stirring up inquiries about Mungo.) When Ted Whitman began to sputter, Tyler sent him along to "show the man." Ted was like a poorly trained small child; you had to give him something to do, to stop his nuisance.

Conrad said he knew the house, so Tyler sent him to the kitchen wing. As he went, Mungo returned with a glass of water. Mungo asked no questions. Tyler stopped himself from thinking that this was odd. It might or might not be. Tyler had to remember to compensate for his own prejudice.

The ambulance boys were enough to take over here, so Tyler gave them the nod, to look after Page and keep the peace. He himself went up the stairs.

The turret room was a weird place. He glanced into its bath, the closet, amused to think that the whole dark prisonlike area was probably thick with Page's fingerprints. That Edith was a spunky one, though. Young, and a little ignorant, as the young are bound to be. But a doer. The Chief rather fancied a doer. He could forgive a lot in a person who did things. Oh, she had a down on her cousin Wendy, that was for sure, and wasn't going to let Wendy Whitman get away with a thing. If *she* could help it. Which she can't probably, thought Tyler. He himself felt almost convinced that Wendy had been the one to battle Myra on Wednesday night. Senseless violence. That was from kooks. And she was a kook, of the purest ray serene. But where had

Mungo been at the time? Tyler wanted to know *that*. And would.

Meantime, what about this housekeeper? A funny one.

He came out of the turret and climbed to the upper balcony. He glanced down into the deep room where Edie and one of the white coats were bending over Harold Page. Wendy Whitman, on the sofa, looked like a squashed by from here.

Tyler knew he couldn't sweep *her* up and tidy *her* away to his jail because she had broken the law. No proof. No evidence. But the family doctor was coming, and Tyler thought that Wendy would be swept up, privately, into some expensive joint and be out of the way for a while, at least. It would be the best that could be done. A female. A rich one. A young one. Even if he had the proof, had the evidence, he thought bitterly.

But Wendy had not been the murderer. He couldn't pin that on her, even in his imagination. Not her style. Nor did he doubt *her* alibi. Oh, she had put Myra into the hospital in the first place. Probably. Into the coma. Somebody hadn't wanted Myra to come out of it. Who? Mungo? Or the housekeeper, maybe?

He wanted that one.

He pushed at a door. Wendy's room. Quite a layout. Bath enormous. Built-in wardrobes. Even a kind of private sunroom overlooking the town.

He looked over his town. Funny, you could see the whole town from here; yet you didn't really see it. It lay there like a . . . well, like a skeleton. You saw where the bones were connected with the bones. But the throbbing flesh, the moving changing blood of it, you could not sense from here.

Not that these people even try, he brooded. They don't notice that they are a part of a world. Go through their lives, getting what they get. How am *I?* That is the question. The hell with what's down there, or out there, or over there—unless and until it begins to bother me.

Many lived like that. Many, rich and poor.

Oh, he conceded that there were loners, natural loners, people who didn't trespass but didn't duck in a crisis, either. They were fine. Some of *them* were fine.

But there are some others—and Charles Tyler, for his sins or his fate, was one of them—who can't help seeing all around, how things flow, how causes affect, and effects cause, and currents cross, and tendencies rise and fall. Can't help trying to *do* something that will improve the whole body. Even if it is only to sweep one town, like a good housekeeper, every day, and in spite of the dust that would settle back, still keep the place at least from being buried under its own filth and rotting entirely.

Now, now, it wasn't a bad little town. *He* watched it. He knew quite a lot that went on under those roof lids—in all-priced houses. But he kept the streets fairly safe and clean, enforcing the laws.

That was his job. He believed in it. You had to have law and the law had to be enforced. That might be the best that you could do, and not quite good enough, but that much *had* to be done.

He could see the Whitman gates from here. A bit of a crowd accumulated? Oh, sure. He wouldn't be sitting on this nest of snakes all by himself for much longer.

Well, put the boy in the hospital—for his own protection, if for nothing else. And apprehend the murderer. He sighed, turned.

Guest room. Bare. Hall closet. Nothing. He started down.

Harold Page was having a vision. He felt pretty groggy. They said he was running a pretty good fever. He guessed he must be. Sunk in the chair . . . would it be forever? . . . he kept seeing the common room at the hospital, his hospital, and the people in it. It was a pattern and not a pattern. You'd think, at first, that it was just an ordinary bunch of people.

But the difference was, each person there was a bead, sliding on its own string. It might look as if the threads were crossing, the beads touching, clustering, attracted or repelled. But it wasn't so. (Like a boy and girl could get married and all, and yet not really touch.) Well, those poor people at the hospital, each was a separate bead, sliding on his own thread, and each was very lonely and frightened.

Until the doctor came. And then the doctor, who was trained and who would know how . . . then it was as if the beads would melt and give a little. Or, the poor people would awaken to where they were and who else was there. So the pattern made a little something.

He sure hoped that he could get to be a doctor. He wondered whether he ever would. He would *like* it, very much.

Nobody moved here. Nobody spoke. Nobody connected.

Except Edie, who was trying to smile cheer and comfort to him. Harold smiled at her.

* * *

Conrad said, "No housekeeper anywhere out this way, sir." Tyler had met him in the dining room.

"You check with your man on the back, whether she left the house?"

"Thought of that." Conrad appreciated Tyler's competence. "Malone *was* on the dining room corner, all right—only you sent him down to the gates."

"Then she could have gone out the back way."

"Could have. Probably did. But . . ."

"Take a look in the cellar," said Tyler practically. "Try the outside cellar door. Maybe they heard her getting out that way." But why? he wondered.

"Right, sir. But there's something I got to thinking . . . Excuse me. The truth is, the Page kid hasn't got a perfect alibi."

"That so?"

"I don't think so. Not if it could have happened, at the hospital, around midnight? Not much later?"

"That's close. Go on."

"Well, right about then, was when I heard this dame screaming, inside. So I come in. It was only the Whitman girl, blowing her top. But see, *then* is when I searched the round room, the one halfway up. And there was nobody to see the front door, except the—what's her name, Edith?—the one who's on Page's side all the time."

"How long were you off guard?" Tyler was quick.

"Five minutes, anyhow. That's time for him to slip in the front door. Murray, on the other corner, mightn't have seen. Fact, see . . . he wasn't supposed to cover the front door. I was. So I just thought . . ."

"Uh huh," said Tyler.

(Yep, that kind of case. Timetables. And one hell of a lot of psychology, he thought gloomily.)

"What was she blowing her top about?" he asked.

"The Whitman kid?"

"Well, I . . . uh . . . was a little late getting in. So I dunno." Conrad looked earnest. "I wasn't too sure what Mr. Whitman would want me to do."

Tyler didn't condemn him for being a hired hand, which he was.

Conrad was enjoying himself. He liked making reports. He liked not having the responsibility. But sounding sharp. It didn't cross his mind that he had forgotten something.

In the big room, nobody moved. Nobody spoke. And it could not hold. Edie had a gone feeling, as if she'd had a tip that something terrible was going to happen, very soon.

Then Granny, with a languid motion of her arm, held up the empty glass and Ronnie Mungo, for his manners, moved helpfully and took it from her. He put it on the table at the end of the sofa. It clicked on the wood. And Wendy convulsed. She bounced to sit up. Her hair was a great tangle. Her eyes looked hot. Immediately, there was a force loose, and what it would do, no one could know. She sent one wild look around.

Granny could *see,* and her pale hand came up and her chin up, and it was an order. So Ronnie Mungo — who had constituted himself Granny's aide-de-camp, somehow — with a closed obedient look on his face, bent over and touched Wendy on her nape.

Wendy was on her feet, like a rocket. "Who touched me?" she screamed. "Who touched me?"

Chapter Sixteen

Mrs. Beck was roused from stupor to alarm at the piercing sound of Wendy's voice.

Oh, no, no! No, no! She knew that note. What could she do? How could she stop it? She twisted, and lifted, and pain was brutal, but her hand got all the way up to the knob.

Ronnie moved to take hold of Wendy but she went whirling. She whirled back. "Ronnie . . ." A high shrill hysteria. "Let's go. *Why* can't we go?"

But now Granny had her ears turned on. "Wendy, you absolutely cannot elope. It would *not* do, at a time like this. Will someone kindly give that child a pill or a shot or something? Where is Dr. Brewster? I called him hours ago. Where is Mrs. Beck, for pity's sakes? We *pay* the woman. Teddy . . . ?"

Ted had come out of the east wing, blinking.

"We couldn't find Mrs. Beck, Mother," he said, querulously, and then, "Charles?"

Wendy whirled. Tyler was there. Conrad, behind him, was poised, watching, with his hand on the knob of the cellar door.

Wendy spun. She threw out her right arm, taut, to its fullest extension. "Look! It's the *madman!* He's *inside,* Daddy! Don't let him hurt me anymore!"

She ran. In panic. Her small feet were quick in her ridiculous little shoes. She ran straight on, toward Harold. She veered. She ran toward the two men in white coats, who waited respectfully at the bottom of the foyer steps. She veered, reversed, and ran up the stairs.

Ronnie had been drawn after her. He called up, standing under the balcony, "Oh, come off it, Wendy," like a man who had had enough, and more.

Wendy shrilled down. "You all don't think he's dangerous? Well, you are *stupid! All* of you!"

Wendy ran on upward, a flash of bright blue, vanishing like a brilliant bird in flight.

Or a bright bead, sliding . . .

And Granny screamed.

The light was bright enough to hurt, when the man opened the door and Mrs. Beck slumped forward. There was a commotion. Seemed like a lot of men. Her arm, her whole side, hurt like sixty. Two of the men were like doctors. She didn't quite pass out under their ministrations. She knew she'd better not. Oh, it didn't hurt to play as weak as she liked, until she saw a chance. Or saw whether she *had* a chance—as she thought she might. After all. After all. If you're lucky—and if you are shrewd, of course, besides.

Then they were trying to put her on a stretcher, but she fought that. She didn't want to be lying down, flat. She wanted to *see*. So they finally had her on her feet, the two of them practically carrying her. One of them had done something, so her arm wasn't quite so draggy on the pain.

She tried to look, to see what was what. Wendy wasn't here. She knew that. Which was good, probably. It was Wendy who mattered. Mrs. Beck could handle all the rest of them. Easily, she thought, with contempt.

Now, she could see the madman, over there. He had his eyes shut. So they had him. The old lady had screamed; now she just sat and trembled. Let her. She didn't matter much. Mr. Whitman was there, looking as if he didn't know enough to come in out of the rain, which he didn't, in her opinion. *He* didn't count. There was Edith, and Edith said, "Mrs. Beck, it was Wendy who fought Myra. Wasn't it? *Please,* say so."

Then Myra's brother yelled, "I'm in charge here." Mrs. Beck thought, *They don't know a thing.*

"We'll get you to the hospital and you'll be looked after, right away," the Chief of Police was saying, in a stern, but respectful manner. "But do you think you could answer a question or two?"

Mrs. Beck had had her clue and wanted nothing better. "I can answer," she said stolidly. (After all, there was only one thing to say.)

Tyler said, "Did you fall, Mrs. Beck?"

"I was pushed," she said.

"How did it happen?"

"I thought I heard something." (She'd keep Wendy all the way out) "So I went to see. But I made a mistake." (That's right, she had—but all was not lost yet) "The madman was in the house, all right. But he was behind me."

"He pushed you?"

"That's right, sir."

(Mrs. Beck saw Edith sit down on the ottoman with a kind of funny smile on her face. Well, pooh to her, thought the housekeeper.)

The other man (one of the guards, she remembered) said, "That cellar door was locked, sir. Unlocked it myself, with Mr. Whitman's key. She couldn't . . ."

"Lock it from the outside," said Tyler. "Right." He began to clear a way, until Mrs. Beck could plainly see the madman, who opened his eyes and looked up at her with a funny expression. Kind of a steady, sad look.

"Do you know this man?" barked Tyler.

"Yes, sir. That's him. That's Harold Page." And the madman tipped his head, like he was listening hard for something she wasn't saying.

The guard said, "Excuse me. Mr. Whitman's gun is down there. Cellar floor."

"Why is that?" Tyler said.

(But this was easy.) "Well, sir, *I* took it, because we all knew how dangerous he was. But he got at me from behind. Tried to kill me, I guess." She played fading out weakly. (But I don't kill so easy as some, she thought to herself.)

"All right. Now, we'll get you taken care of."

Tyler was in charge. The men wanted her on the stretcher. So Mr. Mungo and the guard fellow were holding it. Mrs. Beck let herself be tilted and lifted up. All right, she was hurt. Let them make a fuss over her.

Oh, Mrs. Beck knew she was riding on the wind. It all depended on whether Wendy would keep her mouth shut. But one thing, for sure, they were both in it, and if one told, the other had something to tell, too. Mrs. Beck was not consciously a philosopher, but a principle that she believed appeared (although not as such) in her mind. Everybody looked out for himself first. Naturally. So that was what *Wendy* would do. Barring one of her fits, that is. But Mrs. Beck had hope that all would be well. She would get

202

back as soon as she could. Who knows? Maybe right away, with a cast on. The old lady never listened to anybody. Mr. Whitman never *did* anything. They'd probably dope Wendy up, or get the doctor to do it. It would be all right. She was feeling lucky.

She saw one thing, as she was sinking down. The madman was looking sorry for her. Well, he better be sorry for himself, she thought. And put him out of her mind. He was mad. He didn't count. Nobody would listen to him.

But when she saw Mr. Mungo's face, right close, she couldn't help murmuring to him, "Tell Miss Wendy not to be afraid. Be *sure?* Becky will be back to take care . . . Tell her? Poor lamb."

Mr. Mungo ducked away and said to the men, like the gentleman he was, "Easy. Easy. Here, let me open the door for you."

Mrs. Beck lay back, cozy to the pain.

Edie watched them go, without having said a word.

She had just heard an enormous lie. She knew, of her own sure knowledge, that Harold hadn't pushed the housekeeper down the cellar stairs. She, herself, had left Mrs. Beck in the kitchen and gone to him.

She guessed she knew who *had* done it. (Screaming and shaking and crying that somebody was in the tree!) Wendy must have done it. Just then. No wonder, that shaking! But why Wendy had tried to kill her slave and worshiper, Edie could not imagine.

She had given up any more screaming—for herself. She felt stunned by the weight of the truth of this house, that must fall. Must fall.

She realized that Tyler had his eye on her. He said crisply, "I've got to do what I've got to do."

"I know." She knew. Another accusation against

Harold Page. Enough and more, to hold him. She would give her testimony later, in due course, in good time, and proper order. It would still be her word against Mrs. Beck's. No proof. Her word and Harold's, if his could only count.

Tyler seemed to flush. Did he *want* her to fight, now? "I'm holding him for Myra, too," he said. "Suspicion of murder. There's a hole in his alibi."

"No," she said, wonderingly.

"*You* proved he was inside, all right," Tyler said, almost angrily, "in time to have a go at Mrs. Beck. But last night, the guard came off the front door and searched your room. Did you let Page in then? After he'd been busy in the hospital?"

(Damn it, thought Tyler, *I'm* playing the game. The timetables, the loopholes, the ins-and-outs of opportunities. And it's flimsy. The truth is, and always was, *some people wouldn't do some things.* Which is not evidence.)

Edie said, "No, sir, I did not."

Her passivity annoyed him. He said, "We'll take a chance and let the patrol car get Page where he's going."

"That's okay," said Harold Page, almost eagerly.

But Tyler went to the mantel and stared at the water glass. He snapped at the other uniformed man, who had reappeared from the east wing at last. "Go get Jansen. Then take Page. And I want Edith Thompson down at the station for further interrogation. Now. And I want Mungo, too."

"Yes, sir."

Tyler turned and snarled at Edie. "No more questions?"

"Well, there's one," said Edie, almost listlessly. "May Harold please have his shoes on? Cousin Ted,

204

you know where his shoes are." She saw Tyler blink surprise.

"Shoes?" said Cousin Ted. "Oh. Yes. Certainly." He wiggled to his feet. "Oh dear, I forgot, Charles. Found them in the turret room. And that's how we knew . . . er, something. I — I forget. But I do know exactly where I put them. Yes. I'm sure I do."

Cousin Ted went off to his own quarters. Granny, outraged by all these indignities, had obviously turned off her hearing aid again and was stony in her chair.

"I'll get my things?" said Edie to the Chief, half-question, half-announcement.

He nodded, gloomily. As she started up the stairs, she saw him turn and stare again at the water glass.

Doesn't mean a thing, Edie conceded. Not now, when they have discovered a time when Harold could have come in, and then put his prints on the glass, or anywhere else, at any time between midnight and morning.

She didn't get it, Tyler was thinking. She missed that one. She missed two points about the shoes. One, *we* searched, after Myra was found, and they sure weren't here then. Two . . . *Augh!* He shook his big head. Order, he had to have. And would. Order and reason he would have and reason would go to work.

He supposed he'd take the glass. He didn't need it.

He thought, A glass of cold water she gave a hot and thirsty boy, on a hot day — because it figures. There are some things that some people *will* do. And you *know* it, but it's not evidence.

Well, get on with it. Better tell the old lady what's up. He crossed swiftly.

Edie saw him cross and heard Granny say, "I will not listen, Charles. I cannot and I will not budge, either."

I guess you can't, thought Edie sadly.

She went into the turret room to get her things. What things? Couldn't think. Purse? Wrap? Toothbrush? Nightwear? Anyway, she was leaving.

It was sad, in a way. These people were the only ones of her blood in the world. But she had put herself against them and there she would always be, even when the truth came out.

Oh, it would come out. In questions and answers. In long ordeal. The newspapers. The time it would take. The torment. The tarnish. And now another charge. Edie's word and Harold's word against Mrs. Beck's, now. Against the victim's word? Who *protected* Wendy?

Wendy was sacred? No law for her? *She* could push a woman down stone stairs and the woman would protect her? The family would protect her. The money would protect her. Her youth, her looks, her childish will. Her very callousness would protect her.

No, no. Not forever. Sooner or later, in a courtroom if need be—somewhere—the law must be for Wendy, too. *Some* law.

She rummaged in her dresser drawers. What did you take when you didn't know where you were going, for how long? In fact, she snatched up her purse and took her light coat off its hanger.

When she stepped out upon the balcony and closed the wooden door softly behind her, she knew that Granny was still haughtily deaf, and silent in the chair. Cousin Ted not there at all, and no cop in uniform, either. Harold waiting, slumped on the chairarm, heavy of head. Tyler was standing at the steps to the foyer, with his back to the stairs.

But all of them faded from her attention.

Wendy was poised, halfway down the lower right. And in the heaviness of the silent air, Wendy said, in the wheedling, little-girl's voice she knew how to use when she wanted it, "Who was that, Uncle Charles?"

Edie saw Tyler turn, with a swift defensive motion, to look at her. He did not speak. (He was no uncle of hers, thank God!)

Edie had said nothing and made no noise but Wendy suddenly turned her head far around and looked up at her.

Little Wendy. Her grown body, handsome in the bright blue. Her hand, tight on the iron rail. Her dark hair swirling. Her face, her pretty, vicious face, and her lost and terrible eyes . . .

Tyler was thinking, in quick flashes. *This* kook knew what was down cellar. Jumpy as a cat! Did Mungo know, too? Didn't he take the trouble to give me his *alibi* for this pushing? But the point is . . . my point . . . did Mungo or the housekeeper do it to Myra? *One of them* wasn't going to have Myra telling the truth about Wendy Whitman. Now, why not? And which one? I have to hold the Page kid. In the face of what I've got, I have to do that. But this Wendy could tell me what I want to know.

Will I get at her? Using an assault charge, say? Nope. Let me take one step . . . and psychiatrists, three deep. Prominent family. They can afford it. The best "understanding" that money can buy. Oh, the headshrinkers may wrap it up some day and give it to me for a lollipop. I don't want to wait. What's to be done?

Then Wendy said, "Why won't you tell me it was Becky? I saw her. On a stretcher. What's the matter, Uncle Charles? Please?"

Tyler kept looking up at her, now very intent and concentrated. Intuitive in spite of himself, he had the inspiration to say nothing.

So Wendy twisted. Edie looked down into those eyes, calm and intent. There was a sudden bond between her and the big policeman, as strong as iron. He had not spoken. Neither would Edie speak. *There was a law.*

Wendy twitched, twisted to look down again. She was pinned in beams of silent deep attention. She drew a nervous breath. "Harold?" she said on a rising whine.

But it was too late. The boy was half-unconscious. She couldn't reach him. Not anymore.

And heavy must fall.

Wendy pulled herself into a pouting chiding mood. "Oh, Uncle Charles, you're not believing what *she* said? Why, she's just lying!" Tyler did not move an eyelash. *"Becky* is."

Now Wendy fluttered down toward him, and he watched with a cold heart. Sex-kittying will get you nowhere, either, he thought, but it felt sad.

"I didn't push her," cried Wendy, hitting his sad silence like a wall. "Whyever would I push Becky down the cellar stairs?"

Chapter Seventeen

She was the destroyer. Now, they watched her destroy.

Wendy went whirling on the carpet to her grandmother. "Granny, *you're* not going to believe what some stupid servant says about me?"

But Granny had one little hand curved to shade her eyes. She made no response. She hadn't heard a word.

"But she's a murderess!" shrieked Wendy. "You can't believe *her.*"

Cousin Ted came out of the east wing, with Harold's shoes in his right hand. He stopped in his tracks.

"Daddy!" cried Wendy. "She is. She is. She is. She told me."

Ted Whitman, in the limbo of total incomprehension, giggled. It was a terrible sound. Wendy reeled.

But Granny had seen her, now, and leaned forward. "Go upstairs to your room," she said commandingly. "The doctor is coming to see to you."

"But she told me," wailed Wendy, drifting, pleading. "How she got into the hospital, with her white uniform and everything. *Becky* did."

Tyler was pulled a few steps toward the middle of

the room. But then he stopped and simply stood and listened. His face accepted nothing. His instinct knew. Edie was frozen on the balcony.

"She even made a nurse's cap," said Wendy, "to fool them. And she did something to Myra. She *told* me. *I* didn't know she was going to do it."

Out in the driveway, Dr. Brewster's car had pulled up. He was in the ambulance where he had taken over and was expertly attending to Mrs. Beck's arm and shoulder. Ronnie Mungo stood by, as if to be helpful.

Inside, Wendy Whitman was attending to herself.

"*I* didn't push her. *He* did. Harold did. He was in the house. Edie let him in, so it's *her* fault."

Now the girl, in her bright blue, with her hair flying, was turning and turning in the middle of the floor, turning to each person in succession and none of them spoke to her.

(Harold Page was in a nightmare, he thought, probably.)

"But Becky didn't *know* he was in the house, you see? And that's why she thought it must be me. That's why she said that."

The housekeeper had not said "that."

"What's the matter?" screeched Wendy at all the silent faces. "I tell you she is lying! She's a common murderess!"

Her eyes began to roll. She seemed to grow sly. "Oh, you don't know, but she was going to *kill* him. Kill him, too." Wendy was pointing at Harold Page. "She took Daddy's gun. And she was going to kill him. She said, 'Put it on the madman.' She said

210

'Put it on the . . .' "

Tyler seemed to sigh. She glanced at him, the wheels whizzed in her pretty head, behind her sick and evil eyes.

"I didn't want her," Wendy said, like the old Wendy, willful and petulant. "I didn't feel like taking *her*. What would be the use of going away, if *she* came, too?" Then her prancing feet were still and she began to shake her head from side to side, and her hair flew. "Oh, she shouldn't have done that to Myra," said Wendy with grave disapproval. "*I* didn't say she should."

She looked up at Edie and stamped her foot. "Don't you understand? Becky just wants to get *out* of this whole *mess!*" cried Wendy. "That's all she wants. She doesn't care *what* she says!"

It was a nice description of Wendy's own behavior. But nobody spoke.

"Look," the lost girl said, suddenly woeful, "how she beats me. Becky is so mean. You don't know." Her right hand went to her left forearm and began to twist at the flesh through the thin blue fabric. "She often beats me. Look at the marks." The hand clawed under the chin. "See what she does? Daddy, please don't let her beat me anymore?"

Harold was closing his ears to echoes, his heart upon the pain he thought he dreamed again.

Edie thought, Oh no, no more! But was still. It held.

Until Ronnie Mungo came dashing in; Tyler turned. Ron said, "Excuse me. Dr. Brewster is out there with Mrs. —"

"Ronnie?" said Wendy. Her voice became gruesomely gay. Her body became seductive. She sidled toward him. Tyler stepped out of the way. (The big man looked ill.) "Ronnie, there you are, darling.

211

Why don't we just go, now? It's perfectly all right. Nobody believes what Becky says. She is just a crazy old fool. So we can go to Mexico and be married and go to Paris—and everything?"

Ronnie Mungo's foot went back and groped for the step to the foyer.

"I told you I didn't care," said Wendy, walking toward him with her hips swaying. "If you and Myra were shacking up once, why should I care about that? *She* cared. Myra didn't want me to have you." Wendy giggled. "She was stupid."

Ronnie was looking down at her as if he saw a serpent. Cousin Ted plopped into a chair. Fallen.

"But she's dead, now," said Wendy gaily.

Then Wendy seemed to know that this world was not going to be with her. That she was all alone, in some other. "I didn't mean . . ." She looked around in terror. "I didn't mean . . ." Her arms flew up. "I-never-did-mean-anything," said Wendy, in a different voice, with a great deadening. And with a seeping out of all her false, bright, desperate force, she began to fall.

Ronnie caught her. He said, over her head to Tyler, "What shall I do with her?" as if she were rubbish.

Harold Page had lifted his head. His skin was tight to the bone and of the bone's color. But he made no sound.

The doctor came into the house. They took Wendy to the foyer, as if these men, not members of the family—the doctor, the policeman, and even Ronnie Mungo—knew that the sight and sound of her, now, was better hidden.

Edie went quietly back into the turret room. She hunted in the folds of her peignoir and found what she was after.

212

When she came out, the doctor was consulting with Granny. He was a middle-aged man with a soothing manner and a nervous, realistic eye. "Can't handle it here. You really should not try, Mrs. Whitman. I don't advise it. You must think of yourself."

"This place you speak of," said Granny briskly, "is it respectable? We can afford what it costs, of course."

Edie went down the lower flight and up into the foyer and around the corner of the wall. They had put Wendy on a silly little Victorian settee. Edie did not look at her. She looked at Tyler, whose eyes met hers with patient courage. She held out to him the paper napkin, folded and pinned, to make a boat or a hat. Or a nurse's cap.

"This is for you," she said gravely.

Tyler took it. Understood. Nodded. Did not smile. Went swiftly out the front door to where the ambulance waited, on his orders, for him to come.

Edie heard Wendy's little-girl's voice saying to the young cop, whose back was stiff to his duty and whose face was not telling how he felt, "I was always pretty." She sounded like a child, a real one, beaten and miserable, hunting for one tiny grain of assurance, some one little good thing, from which to take a taste of pleasure, a bit of the nourishment of pride.

Edie stumbled back into the big room, passing the doctor, who was hustling out of it. Cousin Ted had not moved. He lay in the chair as he had fallen, looking like the frog-footman. Edie went to him and gently took from his unresisting hand the shoes. Her brain began to move with a jolt.

Harold's shoes. Well! She would hardly have been letting him in at the front door at the very moment that his shoes were being found in her room. But his alibi didn't matter anymore.

She knelt before Harold, with the shoes. He bent and took them from her. He fumbled at the laces. Edie guessed that he would like to hide his face, so she rose and walked apart.

Outside, Tyler had made short work of Mrs. Beck. He had the paper hat. He had the news that Wendy was talking, which the woman had feared, and therefore quickly believed. She agreed, vindictively, that *Wendy* had pushed her down the stairs. (Tyler had not doubted it.)

Wendy was out of his hands, but off his streets. He hadn't much fear that Wendy would be back. Soon or ever. It seemed to him that it was very late, too late, for her. And she hadn't killed his sister. Now he bent his skills upon the one who had, and Mrs. Beck soon began to boast about her method. He was able to refrain from touching her. He told the men to take her away. He had "gotten" enough to arrest her. He would get more, much more. He would "get" her, solidly, beyond the shadow of a doubt. He didn't think that Mrs. Beck would go to the chair. But *she* would be off the streets, he vowed. Forever. That was his job, wasn't it? To enforce the law, and protect the innocent, as early as he could.

Then he said to Mungo, who was hanging around, "All right. Let's get down to it. Did Myra threaten you?"

Mungo was trying to look blank, but Tyler wasn't having any of that. "Did she threaten to tell about your affair and bust up your impending marriage?"

"No, sir, she did not," Mungo said, his tanned

ce switching over to earnest honesty, now that he
new that Tyler knew.

"She was there Wednesday night. You spoke to
Myra."

"Yes, sir. I've said so." Under Tyler's icy eye,
onnie went on. "The fact is, Myra tried to . . . er
. . convince me that it wasn't a good idea to
arry Wendy Whitman. She was right, I think."
onnie flew one eyebrow.

"And . . . ?" Tyler used his terrible patience.

"Well, sir, Wendy didn't much like that. You
e"—now there would be the confidence, man to
an—"that's why *I* was so sure that Page hadn't
ot in, as they thought. Wendy was spoiling for
me kind of battle when they . . . er . . . put me
ut."

"And you went?"

"Yes, sir." Mungo tried on his charming grin,
arefully seasoned with a touch of rue.

"So nothing was said about your past association
ith my sister? How did Wendy know it?"

"Well, in fact, it was Wendy who did say some-
ing. On Wednesday. She seemed to know all
out it, and said she *had* known for a long time
. . and couldn't care less. You . . . er . . . heard
er."

"How did she know?"

"I can't say, sir. Wendy was wild at Myra for be-
g what she called a 'hypocrite.' " Then Mungo
dded, with a touch of noble sternness, "But she
as wrong. Myra was a good friend of mine, I
ink. And I'm sorry."

"But you didn't think fit to tell me your strong
uspicion? Who had knocked your good friend
own."

Mungo had an odd look. As if to say, "Come

215

now, really!"

"Because you had to marry the money, eh?" snapped Tyler. "You couldn't offend it. You neede the money bad, from what I hear."

"I did and I do," said Ronnie and shrugged. H looked bleak.

"Why did you stick your neck out, trying tha fool stunt of getting Page out of here? You don seem the type to stick out a lot of neck—to me."

Ronnie said rapidly, "As soon as I heard tha Myra was dead . . . and *I* thought it was from th injuries that Wendy had . . . er . . . probabl caused . . . Well, I knew it was going to blow *Wendy* was going to blow, I mean."

Tyler thought he was being somewhat honest, a the moment.

"So there was this kid Page. *I* knew he was jus unlucky. In fact, I knew all about what they ha done to him before. So, when a damsel in distres appealed to me . . ." Ronnie began to look uncom fortable. "That's about all I can say, sir. If I said felt like being the Good Samaritan, on an impulse you wouldn't believe it. Call it a challenge. I didn' . . . think it through."

"I'll call it," said Tyler dryly. "Let me see. Th Whitman money. Myra wasn't going to get it—be ing dead. Wendy wasn't going to get it, or he mother's money, either—being nuts. Ted will have t be a kind of ward of the estate when old Mrs Whitman goes. He'll never be in charge. The on (you thought?) who will get all of it . . . (and thi came to you like an uncontrollable impulse, eh? . . . that one is Miss Edith Thompson. And ther she was. In distress, too. Why let her get disinher ited? Recoup your losses. Right?"

But Edith is too smart for *him,* thought Tyle

216

confidently.

Ronnie said hastily, "But old Mrs. Whitman wasn't —"

"Dead," snapped Tyler, "and isn't, yet. Also, it slipped your mind there's a baby who is an heir. Forgot? Oh, you didn't think it *through* — I guess."

Tyler half turned away. He had better not touch this fellow. But then swiftly, he turned back and pounced. "Now, you tell me how you knew what they had done to Page before. You mean at the time of the divorce? This beating? Nothing got around. I didn't hear it."

"No, sir, it was a simple divorce action on the grounds of 'mental cruelty.' Not that detail — the way it worked out. But they clobbered him with it, just the same. He had no chance. Wendy lied when she said he beat her, and Mrs. Beck lied herself blue to back that up. The Whitmans . . . er . . . chose to believe them. Page had to go quietly."

"But you knew all about it? Who told you?"

"Oh . . ." Ronnie blinked. "Why, Myra told me."

"When?"

"Why, at the time." Ronnie saw nothing amiss.

"I see," said Charles Tyler heavily. At the time, Myra had been engaged to the Whitman money. Hadn't offended it with the truth. Her brother's bitter sorrow came out in anger. "You also knew that Beck was down cellar, maybe hurt. Didn't you?" he roared.

"No, sir. No, sir."

"Come on."

"I thought I heard something. I didn't *know*."

"You need a little practice in Samaritanism, wouldn't you say?" said Tyler, with bitter contempt.

"Sorry," said Mungo, slipping out from under, the voice light, the eyes curious. (Why do you care,

217

hurt or not? Especially when now you know she killed your sister. The foxy eyes were wondering.)

"What a specimen you are," said Tyler. "Get in there. Tell Page he is free to do what he wants, will you? So long as I get his statement tomorrow. And Edith, too."

"I'll be very glad to, sir," said Ronnie Mungo smoothly.

Charles Tyler thought, He's one of those. He isn't glad. He isn't sorry. Doesn't judge, of course — not he. Wouldn't get that much involved. Laissez-faire. Wouldn't help the wronged — without profit in sight. Or the suffering. Doesn't dream of stopping the wicked. Wouldn't have the word in his vocabulary. One of those.

And so had his sister Myra been . . . one of those.

He reached, in pain, for charity. Perhaps not totally. She hadn't cared what happened to Harold Page. But maybe she *had* been a good friend of Mungo's. Maybe, for him, she had made one try. He didn't know. There might have been that one flash of concern for another living person. At *some* risk to herself. She had died of it. Tyler had doubt, but he would give her the benefit. She was dead.

Deliver us? he said, beneath his breath. Then . . . went about his business.

Chapter Eighteen

In the big room, Granny was saying, "Dreadful woman, putting such nonsense into little Wendy's head. Such *vulgar* lies about poor Myra. Well, she's gone. We have arrangements to make, Ted. Will you speak to Charles about the funeral, or shall I?"

Ted stirred. His mother had told him what to think and gratefully he began to think it. "Lies. Dreadful. Poor sensitive little Wendy. No wonder she was upset! Did I"—Ted seemed to lose his grip entirely for a moment—"tell you that Myra is dead? Oh. Well. Yes." His mother had also told him what to do. "We must, of course, make the arrangements. Don't worry, Mother. I'll see to everything."

He was like a balloon that had partially collapsed but now received new air. He got up and trotted toward the foyer. Wendy wasn't there now. They had taken her outside.

"Ted?" called Granny after him. "Teddy? It would be best not to speak to any newsmen."

Ted turned on the steps. He touched his eyebrows with an arched hand. "Oh, Mother . . . I am not *absolutely* stupid."

Poor man, thought Edie, I rather hope that he is.

When Ted was gone, Granny got up with spry energy. "A great deal to attend to," she muttered. *She*, of course, would see that somebody saw to everything.

"Can I help you?" said Edie, without thinking about it.

"I think not, Edith," said Granny, with a frosty look. "I shall go to my room. As soon as my lawyer arrives, I shall be able to manage. After all, I retain him."

She started toward the east wing. Nothing could be given her. She hired what she wanted.

Harold was still bent over, one shoe on, his fingers awkward on the laces. Granny halted to look down at him. A frown creased her pale forehead. "I have always been generous," she said. "No one can say . . ."

For a moment, Edith thought the old lady would break under the weight, but Granny did not. "*I* am paying for that child's special education," said Granny briskly. "Later on, I suppose there are persons who can be employed to look after him."

Oh no, you can't! You can't, thought Edie. Oh, you poor old woman, you can't do that!

Ronnie Mungo came bounding in. "The doctor thinks it best to take Wendy along, right now, Mrs. Whitman, while she—er—isn't minding what they do. I am sorry. Very sorry, ma'am."

The old lady was looking at him in her old way, her eyes shifting.

"About Myra and me," said Ron, softly, "I can't imagine where poor disturbed Wendy got such an idea. It is just . . . not true, you know."

"It makes no difference," said old Mrs. Whitman with great conviction and authority, "whether it is true or false, as long as you don't mention it."

She swept away. Her creed, thought Edie, and seemed to have a revelation. Lila Whitman was the source of the evil in this house. Cruel and lazy. Supping with the devil, by a spoon not long enough.

But she was gone and Ronnie Mungo turned to the two of them who were left, with a resumption of jaunty good cheer. "Mrs. Beck broke down, all right. Tyler was too much for *her*. So Tyler says to tell you" — now, he addressed Harold — "that he'll want your statement tomorrow. But you are free."

"Oh yes. Oh yes. Oh yes." Harold rammed his swollen foot into the other shoe at last, and the pain was fine. It seemed to clear his head. "Thank you," he said.

Edie began to feel fiercely practical. "Will you help me?" she said to Ronnie, demandingly. "I must get him to a doctor and maybe find a place for him to stay."

"You must?" The voice was light, the gaze curious, as if he were examining a species he had not often encountered.

"Will you take us, in your car? And please, catch that Dr. Brewster. Is he still here? Ask him where to go."

Ron was still gazing at her.

Are you weighing, thought Edie, whether it is necessary or advisable, or any special "kick," to help me? "Will you *do* it," she cried, "for *no* reason?"

He said, lightly, "Of course, fair damsel," grinned his mischievous, mocking grin, saluted and started for the foyer.

Then you can run along and play, she said to herself. As if he had heard, Ron glanced back over his shoulder. She felt the curtain falling. He went on.

Edie ran up to the turret room to throw her things

221

into her suitcases. She worked very fast.

Now she could mourn. Myra is dead, who shouldn't have died. And I'm sorry. I'm sorry. I didn't know her, but I do know she shouldn't have been cut down, just cut down by those two. People come in all kinds. But what shall we do with the destroyers? Call them unfortunate? Which they are.

My father labored all his life trying to help the unfortunate. But I am seeing too much destruction, too many unfortunates, rich or poor, who carelessly destroy. How shall we stop them before the compassionate are all their servants, as well as their victims?

Oh, I am not where I want to be, not in the front lines. I want to count, to make a difference, a better difference. I'm doing too little, patching and mending, and failing too often, because it's too late—and too late for too many. Study, then? Find out how? Begin sooner? Work with the new ones, the littlest ones, the ones not lost yet . . . where the chances are? Shall I learn to work with children?

Oh, for that I'll need more patience. I've got the energy, I'm boiling with it, but it needs harnessing. It needs to go where it can feel it matters. That's *my* harnessing. I'm not my long-suffering father and not my patient, easygoing mother, either. I am me . . . and I must do what I can. I wish . . .

I wish I had a man like Charles Tyler. Not he . . . but like him. That is not absurd. Not absurd at all. Not at all.

She came, thoughtfully, out on the balcony with her bags, the big one and the small. Harold Page was waiting down there, all alone.

You didn't get destroyed, thought Edie. Maybe, once, when you were very small, somebody gave you an everlasting clue?

She went down to him. "There's one thing," she heard herself saying. "You'll get to raise your little son, Harold. I'm sure of it. You can win. Could you think about *that?*" She was wishing to lift his spirits, now.

"Yes," the boy said, "I will think about that. In a minute." He looked exhausted. "You don't hate her now, either. Do you, Edie?"

"No," she burst, "but I hate *something.* I hate the rotten misery of spoiled lives. Human beings are not *supposed* to grow up to be such monsters—such dangerous, unhappy monsters."

"Do you think," said Harold as if he hadn't heard her, "they'll figure out what it was that Wendy wanted?"

Edie felt impatient with him. You survived. You have things to do. Get on with it. It was only your bad luck, that Wendy took a notion to run away with you—for fun. But Mrs. Beck "couldn't approve"—so . . .

Then the whole story of Wendy flashed clear into her mind. A baby, here. A little new one. The only child, with a pair of silly parents, in a cold old house dominated by a grandmother who bought everything. Who had hired a woman to raise the child. Who couldn't be bothered, hadn't even noticed, how the servant had become the master, how Mrs. Beck had twisted her own solitary meaningless life around Wendy's, like a strangling poisonous vine.

Oh, pity, thought Edie, to have been born into this. To have been ever indulged, from the beginning, to have escaped justice, to have been denied it, to have lacked it. And then to be forever told, by that powerful, sick hired woman, that nothing so difficult, or so sweet, as a struggling life was for you.

223

She no longer thought that Wendy had run away with Harold Page for fun, or money. But instinctively, for her own salvation. And had not made it. Wendy had been going to marry Ronnie Mungo, not for love nor money, but for her own last chance. He would have married the money. Wendy would have got away. *Anywhere*. To shuck off the past? To go somewhere else, looking for the turning-around place? Too late. Too late. She hadn't made it. Had followed bad with worse, spiraling downward. How could she have made it — all alone — never having had a clue?

"What Wendy wanted?" said Edie aloud. "I think she told us."

The boy was all right. He could take it.

"What she wanted," said Edie, slowly, "was only human. Only human. Wendy wanted to mean something. But she . . . was a prisoner in a tower. Don' you think so?"